# SHADOW OF THE HIDDEN

"*Shadow of the Hidden* takes the reader on a whirlwind and heartrending adventure through Turkey and North Africa, embracing culture, cuisine and curses along the way. A trip of a read! I loved it!"
—Catherine McCarthy, author of *Mosaic* and *A Moonlit Path of Madness*

"Kev Harrison is the master of folklore. *Shadow of the Hidden* takes us on a global thrill ride, weaving in memorable characters and parts of the world horror tends to ignore. I adored it."
—Dan Howarth Author of *Territory*

"In *Shadow of the Hidden*, Harrison constructs a maze of grimy streets, dusty crypts writhing with ancient horrors, and thronging crowds full of leering menace. This one will stay with you."
—Zachary Ashford, author of *Polephymus* and *The Morass*

"Fascinating, richly textured and genuinely unsettling, *Shadow of the Hidden* is a horrifying delight from start to finish—and a refreshing change from the usual horror themes and setting. Highly, highly recommended"
—T.C. Parker, author of *Salt Blood, Hummingbird* and *To Coventry*

"Fast-paced, riveting, and rich with culture, *Shadow of the Hidden* does not pull punches but certainly pulls heartstrings. Harrison weaves together an unsettling yet wondrous story about adventure, friendship, and the ultimate sacrifice backdropped by the beautiful Middle East."
—Mona Kabbani, author of *The Bell Chime, Vanilla,* and *For You*

# Shadow of the Hidden

## by Kev Harrison

Edited by Elle Turpitt

Formatted by Stephanie Ellis

Cover illustration and design by Mustapha Design DZ

First Edition: March 2024

ISBN (paperback): 978-1-957537-94-8
ISBN (ebook): 978-1-957537-93-1
Library of Congress Control Number: 2024932442

BRIGIDS GATE PRESS

Overland Park, Kansas

www.brigidsgatepress.com

Printed in the United States of America

*For my dad, John George Harrison (4th Dec 1954 – 29th January 2022) without whose stories of far-flung travels I'm sure this book and the journeys which birthed it would never have come to pass.*


*I think you would've liked this one, old fella.*

Content warnings are provided at the end of this book

# Part One

# Chapter One

I dropped the two mother-of-pearl dice into the cup and shook. They rattled around, while a cloud of fragrant apple tobacco smoke drifted over from the shisha bar on the opposite side of the cobbled street. I rolled the dice onto the board. Four and three. My cheeks flushed as I grinned and moved my pieces home.

"Did you let me win?" I said, offering Oz my hand. My landlord while working here for the past three seasons, and now firm friend, smiled—all teeth—and shook my hand firmly.

"Not at all. I told you I'd teach you well enough to beat me before you went home."

And he had.

My flight to London via Istanbul was leaving the following day. For four months, I'd been there in that quiet corner of Anatolia, working as linguistic attaché for a French archaeological team. Though this was my third year doing the spring season, this time the discoveries only seemed to mount with each new trench. A Roman fort which had turned out to have Lycian origins. Then an adjoining town, complete with an ornate burial site. My standard two-week contract had turned into four, then eight, before doubling again. Finally, my work was done.

I'd miss the place, of that there was no doubt. After the death of my parents had severed the only real ties I had to anywhere, this place had come to feel like a home of sorts.

Oz packed up the backgammon board and lit the hand-rolled cigarette he'd stashed behind his ear, nestled in his thick black hair. "So tonight, Seb, we party, yeah?"

I stood from the small table, rubbed the cropped hair at the back of my neck. "I dunno, man. I fly out of Dalaman at eight fifteen tomorrow."

He puffed out his cheeks. "Thirty minutes in a taxi. And it's your last night. No excuses!" He looked at his watch. "In fact, it's already six. Beer?"

I sat back down. "Go on then."

"That's my boy." He shuffled behind the bar and grabbed a bottle of Efes for him and a can of Efes Dark for me. He handed me my beer and a frosty glass from the freezer. I rummaged in the pocket of my shorts for my wallet.

"Hey! Stop! Not tonight. Drinks are on me."

"Oz, come on, mate."

He lifted his hand. "Not interested. On me. Besides, no one will drink that shit when you're gone. I have to tell Marie to stop ordering."

Oz had lived in this sun-kissed corner of Anatolia almost his whole life. His parents owned a small farm outside of the town, where they grew citrus fruits, olives, and pomegranates, breeding goats for milk, cheese, and meat. Their eldest son, Enes, now did the majority of the physical work on the farm, but they remained in situ, passing on the knowledge they'd acquired over the decades. It was a simple place, and a simple life.

Things had got a little more complicated, though, when Oz had done his military service in Zonguldak, way up north on the Black Sea coast, and met Marie. A British photographer working in hotels and bars to fund her trip around the country, they'd fallen in love immediately. Oz's parents had been dubious when she'd first moved down. But four years later, they were still going strong.

Oz sat beside me, and we touched glasses. "Çerefe!" we each said and took a drink. I thudded my beer down on the table and sat back against the cushioned wooden bench.

Despite evening's approach, the brilliant blue of the day somehow remained, people beginning to mill into the main street from the few small hotels and apartments on the periphery of the town.

Among the straggle of tourists, a woman stood out. All in black, a heavy veil over her face, she was squat, robustly built, and dragged one leg as she walked. Oz took a long pull on his cigarette, then dropped it into the ashtray at the centre of the table. "Not again," he said, standing and beginning to pace in front of the bar.

"What's up?" I said, concerned. I'd yet to see Oz in a state that fell outside the bounds of calm or humorous.

"This widow. She's been twice this week. Begging for food and stuff."

I shuffled in my seat and lowered my sunglasses to get a better look. "Aren't you supposed to … you know … help widows?"

"Don't start. Marie said the same on Thursday. But she always wants luxury stuff. Won't take bread or cheese."

She ambled closer, then paused, leaning over the ice cream trolley. It shifted on its castors, creaking under her weight.

She spoke to Oz in a pained tone, gesturing wildly toward the sun as it arced downward, then mock-wiping her brow through the veil. Oz shook his head as he replied to her, crossing his arms then opening them again, fiercely, as if to say 'no.' I turned my head at this point, more than a little embarrassed as the argument intensified.

My eyes found those of the waitress at the shisha bar. She, too, looked more than a little disturbed by the exchange. She hurried back inside with a tray of empty tea glasses.

The old widow's tirade continued for several minutes, before she noticeably changed from Turkish to Arabic. She spat her words, the black lace of her veil moving with the force of her language. Oz backed away, mouth agape.

The woman fell silent.

Oz lowered himself to the ground, back against the wall of the bar, and placed his head in his hands. The old woman partially lifted her veil and spat on the ground at Oz's feet. Then she moved off, still dragging the bad leg.

"What the *fuck* was that about?" I asked, standing and offering Oz a hand up.

For at least a minute, he didn't respond. Didn't so much as flinch.

"Hey, are you okay?" I asked and crouched beside him, placing one hand on his shoulder. His body trembled.

"You d-didn't understand? What she said?" He peeked at me through the cracks between his fingers.

"My Arabic amounts to ordering food and getting directions to the train station. Not my area."

"What she said was something … something that should never be said."

I thought about making a joke at this point, but my friend was clearly shaken. "What exactly *did* she say?"

"I won't repeat it. But it was a kind of … curse. On me, my family … It involved some powerful djinn." He swallowed, and what looked like a tear glistened in his eye.

"Oz, mate. Come on. You're not exactly super religious or anything. It's old fairy tales. And she's obviously a crazy old bat."

"*You* didn't hear what she said about my family." He wiped his eyes. "I should've just given her the stupid ice cream."

"Next time, eh? Now, come on." I hauled Oz to his feet. His breath was still short, his skin paler than its usual olive tone, but I hoped he'd be okay.

"Sorry, man. It's your last night. Marie said she'd hold the fort here this evening. Let's grab some food down by the river then go to the music bar. What do you think?"

Something about the way he delivered his words told me he was still anguished. But what could I say?

"Sounds perfect."

***

Marie, like me, said the old lady was probably mad. Just trying to make trouble or scare Oz to get what she wanted. She offered to handle it the next time she came by to beg. This seemed to calm Oz's nerves and he was more like his old self as we sat at the small restaurant at the riverside.

"So, when are you coming back?" he asked, scooping up half a köfte and some pickled red cabbage with his flatbread.

"Well, I have a speaking event with the French team, in Paris in September, but apart from that I'm a free agent until something else crops up. Perhaps in the spring, when it starts to get warm here and London is still drowning in torrential rain." I sliced through my Adana kebab and took a bite. "Are you feeling okay now? After what happened earlier, I mean. The old woman."

Oz grasped his glass and drained a third of his beer, then wiped his mouth with the back of his hand. "What do you know about djinn?"

"Wishes, lamps. Disney's *Aladdin*, basically." I chuckled.

"There *are* stories like that one. Others where they are simple tricksters, making fun with children, or hiding things. But there are others."

"Others ...?" I raised an eyebrow theatrically.

He leaned across the table and whispered. "Some of them are like your demons. Wicked. *Dangerous.*"

I drank a long swallow of beer. "First of all, they aren't *my* demons. I'm an unbeliever. And secondly, those are just stories. Like hellfire, there to make you behave yourself when you feel like doing something bad." I eyed Oz's beer. "Not working too well, is it?"

Oz finished his food and pushed his plate to one side. "I haven't been to prayers in years. But the djinn still scare me to death."

"What scares *me* to death is that I might not be able to get any decent künefe when I get back to London," I said and signalled to the waiter.

***

Slivers of sunlight were already creeping across my face, dragging me from slumber, when I heard Oz's raised voice outside. I tapped my phone screen. Just before six. I had to be up in a few minutes to get my taxi to the airport. I fought my way out of bed and pulled on some clothes, all the while listening to Oz shrieking from below on the street. I opened the window.

"Hey, what's going on?"

I didn't need an answer. The ice cream trolley had been moved into the middle of the street and unplugged. The sun, which had risen at least an hour earlier, had turned Oz's entire stock to mush. "Look at this! Fucking look!" He tugged at his thick hair, gaze fixed on the trolley.

I closed the window and brushed my teeth before stuffing the last of my things into my suitcase and rucksack. I hurried downstairs and out into the morning sun, sweat already clamming up under my arms.

"How did it get out here?" I said, descending the last few steps.

"How do you think?"

I made a face. How the hell was I supposed to know?

"Wasn't it locked up when we got back las—"

"It's *always* locked up!" he snapped back.

I glanced over at the heavy chain that held it. Open, discarded on the floor. "Someone's opened it. Marie?"

"Why would she? And even if she did … Come. Come here." He gesticulated wildly.

I strode over.

"Move it." He stood aside, hands on hips.

I put two hands on it and shoved. The castors creaked, but the machine barely budged. "It must be two-hundred kilos," I said.

"Two-three-five *empty*. No way Marie can move this thing. It was the fucking—"

"Don't say it." I held up my hand.

"How else do you explain it?"

"I don't know." I paced up and down. Bent to look for some sign of how it could have been shoved from its shady spot at one side of the bar. "What I think is the old widow told her thug sons or nephews or *whoever* to come round and fuck up your ice cream fridge. That's how I explain it."

Oz rubbed his neat beard. "That is the sort of thing that could happen."

I moved over, opened my arms. "I have to get going, mate." Oz closed his arms around me in a bear hug, his wiry frame belying his strength. "Want me to help you push it back into the shade before I go?"

He shook his head. "I have to empty it and clean it before restocking. I'll get Serdar from the shisha place to give me a hand when I'm done."

I moved back to my cases, ready to wheel the big one down the cobbled road to the taxi rank. "So, this is farewell."

"*Güle güle*, my friend." He reached out and we shook hands, before I trundled off to find a taxi.

***

I'd been back in London for about five days, mostly consumed by laundry and making arrangements for my trip to Paris later in the year. Despite technically being early summer, the sky was an oppressive sheet of varying shades of grey. The air was humid, sticky. Public transport was close to unbearable, yet I found myself on a bus, moving staccato along Euston Road.

My phone buzzed in my pocket. I fished it out, to find an incoming WhatsApp voice call from Oz. I picked up, my voice projecting the smile I wore across the airwaves. "Oz, how are you doing, man?"

"Seb, I need to talk to you. Something has … happened." His voice was grave, lifeless.

I put my free hand over my other ear, trying to block out the background noise. "What's the matter? Is it Marie?"

"Marie's fine. It's … it's something very unusual. On my parents' farm. I don't know how to … where are you?"

"I'm on a bus, mate. Sorry about all the noise."

"Are there a lot of people near?"

"It's a London bus. In June. It's rammed."

"I need you to see this. To understand. But the people might be afraid."

I tapped the elderly lady sitting next to me—herself on the phone—on the shoulder and gestured for her to move. She hauled herself up and I squeezed through, mouthing a 'sorry' as I passed her. I double pressed the bell and the bus quickly stopped outside the British Library. "Are you still there?"

"Yes. Are you ready?"

"One second. I'm jumping off the bus … right … *now.*"

"I'm going to hang up and send, okay? Call me back when you've looked. I'm waiting."

The phone clicked off.

I felt weird in that moment. I was standing on one of the country's busiest roads, having just spoken to someone who'd become a firm friend, thousands of miles away.

Somehow everything felt distant. Like the camera on my life had zoomed out and I was watching from some faraway vantage point. I leaned back against the red-brick wall and clutched my phone, waiting for the screen to light up with whatever it was Oz wanted me to see.

Finally, the device vibrated and glowed, notifications cascading one over another. Five messages. I swiped the screen and opened the messages. My hand's passage to cover my mouth was every bit as involuntary as breathing or cell-division.

The first image was a close-up.

One of the milk goats, on its back, legs smashed at the knee joints so it lay spread eagled. The chest was crudely ripped open, a cavity surrounded by irregular, jutting bones. Entrails spewed, seemingly at random, from the bloody mouth that its underbelly had become. The heart was missing.

I retched, but got a hold of myself, choking back whatever substance was trying to evacuate me. I swiped through to the next image. Another close-up; it showed the animal's mouth, filled with a spectrum of blood, from crimson to black, the full length of the mandible visible as the tongue had been hacked away, leaving only a glistening, raw stump.

I hit the button at the side of my phone, blanking the screen to a welcome darkness and allowed my arm to drop to my side. "Fuck me," I said aloud, then began a mental ten count, readying myself for the next image. I clicked it back on and opened the third photo. A close-up of the top of the head. The eyes were burned in such a way that there was no way of knowing that they had ever been there. No tissue remained.

They had been scorched out.

The skin around had been heated sufficiently it had blistered even beneath the course fur these Turkish mountain goats possessed.

Unable to see more, I pressed the call button at the top of the chat window and lifted the phone to my ear.

It had barely rung once when Oz answered. He didn't speak.

"I can't believe what they did to that poor creature," I said.

"How many photos did you see?"

"Three. Quite enough."

"So you didn't see the others?"

"Look, whatever else they did to it, I got the message—"

"The other goats, not the other pictures."

"I'm not sure I follow. They did this to more of them?"

"*All* of them. Eighteen. All the same."

"Who—"

"You know who. Or *what*."

"Oz, look—"

"Don't tell me this is mumbo jumbo."

"Of course, this is … this is horrible. But this is a criminal act. Nothing more tha—"

"Will you help me?"

"Help you with what? The goats? I'm in London, I don't know if I can do anything from here."

"I have the curse. I remembered it. Like the words were imprinted on my memory. I asked the Imam to write it down. He began but stopped. Said he would not. Threw me out. Do you know someone? Someone who knows Arabic? Who knows curses? Will you help me?"

I took a huge gulp of a breath, then: "I'll help you if I can. I'll make a few calls."

"Thank you, my friend."

# CHAPTER TWO

I stood at one of the gleaming new meeting points at Istanbul's Ataturk airport, struggling to believe I was even there. I'd left little more than a week ago, ready to have some down time in London just as summer was arriving. But life has a way of throwing a whole variety of tools into the works sometimes.

The visa desk had been interesting. Re-entering on a tourist visa, after almost one hundred and twenty days' residence on a professional one, had needed some explaining. In the end they'd let me through, but I dreaded the talking to I might have on my way out of the country. Oz was flying up from Dalaman. His flight was delayed by thirty minutes, so I had another hour or so to kill. I ordered a Turkish coffee from the nearest café pod and took a seat.

I pulled out my compact laptop and opened the email from Professor Yılmaz, with her initial suggestions of what Oz's curse might have been. I admired the smooth curvature of the Arabic text, then was sobered by the violence of the translations given below. They ranged from the quaint sounding 'eternity of noxious fortune' and 'miasma of negativity' to the horrific 'possession and harvesting of the mortal soul' or 'administration of a thousand forms of suffering.'

Time flew by as I tumbled down the rabbit hole of links and scriptural PDFs she'd sent me, until the announcement that the Pegasus flight from Dalaman had landed cut through my trance. I packed the laptop into my bag, paid for my coffee and strolled over to domestic arrivals.

The stream of suntanned tourists and youngsters from the south coming to the big city filtered through the gate until finally, Oz emerged. I had to look twice to be sure it was him. His skin was pale, he'd lost a fair amount of weight and his shoulders were hunched. He glanced around, looking unfocussed until he saw me. His lips turned up into something approaching a smile and he lumbered over.

"Oz," I said. "You look—"

"Like shit, I know." He wrapped me in his trademark bear hug, tight enough I heard a bone crunch somewhere in one of my shoulders.

"Tough week?" I asked when he released me.

"My parents, Seb. You should've seen them. In fucking ruins, man. I hope this professor has some ideas."

"I hope so, too. Do you want to grab a coffee or something before we—"

"No. I had some on the plane. Let's just get going, okay?"

"Right you are." I took my phone from my pocket as we hurried through the crowds to the exit and requested an Uber to take us to the university. A driver took my request almost immediately. "Murat in a black Renault Megane. One minute away, come on."

We hurried our pace, moving beyond the city cab station and toward the pick-up zone. As we paced across the road, the aforementioned Megane pulled in and a short, bald man with sunglasses stepped out, giving a little wave in my direction.

"*Merhaba*," I said and climbed into the front passenger seat, keeping my shoulder bag with me. Oz climbed into the seat behind and we moved off.

"University, sir?" said the driver. "You work there?"

"No. We're visiting a specialist. I work in archaeology. Translation."

"Very good. You are welcome."

The car zipped forward and swept onto the main coastal road, the tyres just giving the faintest hint of a squeal as we veered across two lanes of traffic to the fast lane. Horns blasted at us in a variety of tones and intensities. I clutched the handle above me.

"Haha, first time Istanbul?" The taxi driver laughed.

"No, no. I've been here many times. Just never get used to the driving."

He chuckled again. "Everyone is crazy. Inshallah, we get to university with no big crash."

I closed my eyes and released a slow breath. When I opened them again, I saw Oz grinning in the rearview mirror. I turned to him.

"Your face," he said.

"Not even a little bit worried?"

He shrugged his shoulders. "You should've seen the military drivers on the mountain roads. I never prayed so much in my life."

I turned back to face front and marvelled at the chaos.

"Which specialist you see?" the taxi driver asked as he undertook a dilapidated city bus and swerved back in.

"A Professor Yılmaz. I've done some work for her before, but never met in person."

"Don't know. But which department? Where I drop you?"

"Sorry, Antiquities and Religion. It's one of the older buildings, I think."

"I know, yes."

I gazed out across the Bosphorus at the densely packed, tan-coloured apartment buildings on the eastern shore, with the occasional dome shimmering at the head of a palace or mosque. Ferries chugged along, smaller pleasure boats darting between them. Huge cargo ships sailed at an almost glacial pace north, toward their destinations on the Black Sea.

"Here," the taxi driver said, pointing as the car shuddered down the exit ramp, stopping at a set of traffic lights. "The old üniversitesı."

I glanced at my watch and saw we'd made good time, despite Oz's flight delay. We wound our way uphill from the coast and into the university's main parking area. The car came to a stop at the taxi drop off point.

"Perfect, thank you," I said and opened my door.

"One moment," the taxi driver said, leaning over.

"Yes?"

"Not you, *you*." He looked up at Oz, already out of the car and on the pavement. The driver's eyes were clouded.

"You should talk to Sıla, while you still can."

Oz lunged toward the car, bundling me to one side. "What did you say?"

The taxi driver shifted into gear and burst forward. Oz sprinted after him, screaming in Turkish. The man reached out, even as the car turned one hundred and eighty degrees, slamming the door shut, then raced from the car park, narrowly avoiding a truck as he hit the main road.

Oz ambled back to me, fists clenching and unclenching.

"What's happening with Sıla?" I said, trying to remain calm.

"It was in him."

"What was?"

"The djinn. How did he know her name otherwise?"

"A lucky guess? It's not such an uncommon name. Oz, what's happening with Sıla?" I asked again.

"Nothing. As far as I know. She'll be at school now. Let's get through this meeting and I'll call and check on her while she's having lunch."

*** 

We made our way into the domed, Ottoman-style building and began to climb the curved marble staircase. Indentations in each step, recalling many thousands of footfalls, revealed the structure's age. Arriving at the third floor, we pushed through the heavy door into Antiquities.

An administrator looked up at us from behind a computer screen at the desk as we entered. He greeted us warmly in Turkish. Oz stepped forward and explained we were here to see the professor and he immediately switched to English.

"Doctor Mackie?"

"Um ... not doctor, no. The PhD ... well ... it's a long story."

"Mister Mackie, then." He outstretched a hand enthusiastically, which I shook. "Can I get you both some tea?"

I waved away his offer. "I don't think so. This is pretty urgent, and I'm sure the professor is very busy."

"Judging by the resources she's been requesting ahead of your meeting, it must be. Come with me." He moved out from behind his desk and led us down the corridor, past a series of closed doors until we reached Professor Yılmaz's office. He knocked gently.

"*Evet?*" said a firm, enthusiastic voice, almost immediately.

"I have Doc—*Mister* Mackie here to see you."

The door burst inward and Professor Yılmaz stood there in the doorway, wearing a plain turtleneck under denim dungarees, hair in loose, energetic black curls.

"Hi!" she said, with an American-sounding twang. "Come in." She stepped aside and gestured theatrically in the style of a doorman, allowing Oz and I into the room. "Thanks, Emre. If I need anything, I'll call your desk." Emre nodded and backed out, allowing the door to close behind him.

"Sit, please, sit. Did Emre offer you both tea?" she said as she rounded her desk and lowered herself into her seat.

"He did, yes. I think we're okay for now," I said, and sat.

Her desk was littered with books in various positions, all of them ornately decorated, calligraphy in shimmering metallic inks, spines threaded with gold leaf. She clicked and scrolled with her mouse, the screen turned away from us, then stopped.

"Okay then. Here we are." She twisted the screen around to face us. "This is a list of all known curses which are in use that involve the djinn. Oz—it *is* Oz, isn't it?"

Oz made an affirmative sound.

"Great. Oz, can you remember the words this old woman used when she spoke to you?"

My friend cleared his throat. "I can. I remember all. Every word."

"Do you recognise the words from any of these on the screen?" She zoomed in, making the calligraphy bolder, clearer.

Oz shook his head. "I didn't go to mosque in years."

"Okay, then just recite it for me—slowly—and I'll try to transcribe."

He cleared his throat again, his eyes shifting upward as he focussed, then he began to recite the curse.

"Stop. Stop-stop-stop!" Yılmaz was out of her chair, scooping back her hair in her hands and breathing out a long sigh. "Not that one. Shit, not that one. Excuse my language." She began to pick up and close the books from the desk in front of her, stacking them to one side.

"What does it mean? Why are you so ... spooked?" I said.

Yılmaz sat back in her chair.

"Sebastian," she said. "When I said this list was of all the curses *in use*, that's exactly what I meant. There are some curses—mainly those involving the ghul—which are not in use. As in *no one* uses them."

"Please, call me Seb," I said. "Why are they *not* in use, as you put it?" I made air quotes as I said 'in use' and immediately felt like a prick.

Her face twisted into a smile that was anything but happy. To me, it was all rage, packaged in sarcasm.

"When I studied in the US, on my undergrad, I was amazed by all the girls in my boarding house. Their talk of Ouija boards, Bloody Mary—all that stuff. But later, I thought about it. Why *do* people do that kind of stuff? I mean, what's the risk?" She paused, eyes boring into mine.

I glanced over at Oz. He, too, was staring at me.

"Are you asking me?" I said.

"Mmhmm."

"How should I know. I haven't done any of that stuff. Ever."

"A-ha, and why? Why didn't you?"

"Because ..." I swallowed. Glanced at Oz again. "Because what if something *does* happen? Why would I risk it?"

She leaned across the table, her curly hair bouncing exaggeratedly as she did so. "But the risk is calculated. They don't believe anything's going to happen. Not really. It's the same with these." She sat back up and tapped the top of the PC monitor. "No one believes in these. It's why they're written down. They're like the boogie man. For scaring naughty kids. This ..." She pointed at Oz. "This thing with your goats. This is used with intent. To harm. Maybe worse."

Oz's phone blasted loudly to life from his pocket. He slipped it out and glanced at the name: Enes. His brother. "Worse," he said, and left the small office, pulling the door quietly shut behind him and mumbling into the phone.

A moment of silence passed between the professor and I until I decided to break it. "I was really hoping you'd be able to calm him down."

Yılmaz unscrewed a water bottle at the side of the computer and refilled her glass, taking a sip. "I'm not a therapist. Nor a cheerleader. If you didn't want the truth, perhaps you shouldn't have come to see me."

I stroked my chin for a moment, thinking about how to respond. "You're an expert, but you don't *believe* in this stuff, do you? Not really."

"Seb, you sent me that photo. I'm aware of this type of curse, but have never, ever seen or heard of it in reality."

"There has to be some other explana—"

"Oh, yes? How long—and how many men—would you need to do … *that* to more than a dozen goats?"

I didn't respond.

"At this moment, this *is* the simplest explanation."

"So, supposing it is a djinn—a ghul, as you called it. What do we do? What are the next steps?"

She stood and walked over to a filing cabinet, pulling open a creaking drawer. "The easiest way is to find this … this widow. Ask her to retract the curse. If she's in contact with the *ghul*, you should be looking at burial grounds, swamps, places where there have been mass deaths or burials. Failing that, you could talk to this guy." She handed me a paper in a plastic sleeve.

I scanned the details. "Kairouan? Tunisia?"

"Unless you fancy smuggling yourself into Mecca." She made a neck-slicing gesture. "He's the best expert I know of on Islamic exorcism, expelling of djinn and all that projectile-vomit-related stuff."

It took me a moment to realise my mouth was gaping.

"Not really, dangalak."

I laughed at the insult and the fact she articulated it *so* much better than I ever could.

The door opened and Oz walked in. His face was dry, but his cheeks bore the streaks of tears. I stood.

"Hey! You okay, man?"

"It's Sıla. She collapsed at school."

"Is she …?"

"In hospital. A coma. I have to go."

"I'm coming with you," I said, folding the paper with the contact details of the Tunisian cleric into my shoulder bag. I turned back to the professor. "Professor Yılmaz, thank you so much for your time."

She reached her hand across for Oz and then me to shake. "It's my pleasure, really. I'd love you both to keep me posted. You have my email, and my cell number is in my email signature." She moved to the office door, pulling it open. "Good luck, Oz. I hope Sıla is okay. And call me Deniz, please."

"My mother is Deniz, also. *Teşekkür ederim.*"

We thanked Emre again on our way out and then hurried from the building to the main road. Oz began trying to hail cabs from a bus stop.

"What happened with Sıla? What's wrong with her?" I said.

He moved back to me, half an eye on the traffic and his thumb still out into the road. "She just collapsed. Enes said she's normal. Everything normal except the brain waves. Flat. Like a deep sleep."

"I'm so fucking sorry, man."

A taxi slowed and signalled that it was stopping. We hurried over and Oz opened the door.

"You know, it isn't *necessarily* related," I said.

Oz stared at me. "Fucking wake up," he said and got in, slamming the door shut.

# Chapter Three

I'd always hated hospitals and that being the place where Oz's niece lay 'sleeping' didn't do anything to change my mind. I spent most of the evening in the corridor, where nurses brought me endless cups of Turkish tea, served with smiles and encouragement in broken English. Enes, Oz's brother, relayed to him in more detail what the doctor had said about Sıla's condition. Oz then translated for me, as best he could.

I felt useless.

As midnight approached, I took Oz aside. "How is she? What are the doctors saying?"

"The same." He shrugged his shoulders and yawned. "It's the lack of answers which terrifies Enes the most. This place is expensive. He told me he only has the money to pay for this type of care for fifteen days. Then he'll have to ask our parents to sell the farm or …"

"Or?"

"They switch her off, Seb."

Those words held so much gravity, I almost lost my footing. I righted myself, then said, "Look, mate, I'm going to go. I need to get some sleep and I want to do something to help. I want to be useful."

"What you have in mind?"

"I'm going to get up tomorrow morning, head up to the villages in the hills beyond the town. Try to track down this old woman."

Oz glanced through the glass panel in the door at his brother and sister-in-law, sat at Sıla's bedside. "It's a good idea. I'll stay for one more hour. Tomorrow, I come with you." He reached into his pocket, then handed me a key. "The apartment. It's free. Marie will make you something to eat if you need."

"Nah, it's late. She's got enough on her plate consoling your folks. I'll grab a dürüm on the way back. Thank you," I said and hugged him.

***

I woke up not long after dawn, my mouth dry. That's what happens when you eat a chicken kebab roll from the last place open in town just before going to bed. I stretched and went to the fridge, finding the guys had left me a few basics and, mercifully, a bottle of water. I glugged half of it straight down and fired up my laptop.

Digging the paper Deniz had given me with the cleric in Kairouan's details from my shoulder bag, I connected to the apartment's Wi-Fi. Gradually, I cobbled together enough French vocabulary on the subject of curses, demons, and possession to fashion an email, explaining everything from our first encounter with the old woman to Deniz's reaction to the curse and, ultimately, Sıla's collapse.

Satisfied, I hit send and shut down the machine, before dialling Oz's number on my mobile. It had barely rung before he answered. "Oz, I didn't wake you?"

"I barely slept, honestly."

"How's Marie?"

"Better than me. But tired. So tired. My parents left after midnight." There was a long pause, clunking noises as Oz moved around the apartment. "I don't want to wake her. Let's breakfast in the shisha place over the road. They do great *menemen*. Then we'll hire a scooter. Faster. See you downstairs."

The phone clicked off. I quickly cleaned myself up a bit and went down.

Stepping out into the morning sun, I was glad for the protection of the long sleeves of my linen shirt. Oz was already waiting, sitting at a table outside the shisha bar and drawing nervously on his cigarette. The thick, black stubble growing around his usually immaculate beard only accentuated how pale he'd become.

"Hey. You okay?"

"Do I look like I'm okay?"

"You want my honest answer?"

He took one long, final drag on his cigarette and stubbed it out in an ashtray before exhaling, nodding through the haze of smoke.

"You look like death, mate. I'm sorry."

He waved away my apology. "I look like I feel. I feel like my niece is in a black magic coma."

I couldn't argue with that. "You still have an appetite, though?"

He laughed then—his real laugh, which lifted me. "If I lose appetite, it means the djinn found a way inside me and you have to …" He made gun hands and fired into his temple.

A waitress came out of the bar with a tray and a cloth. "Merhaba," she said.

"Want to do the honours?" Oz raised an eyebrow at me.

I racked my brain for the words, just about remembering how to order in Turkish. Oz clapped his hands and the waitress scurried back inside. She re-emerged almost before I had a chance to sit down, placing two empty, ornately handled cups between us, each on a rectangular plate, with a small stack of sugar cubes to one side.

"Coffee will be a minute. You want water, too?" she asked.

"Nevda, he was doing so well," Oz said, winking.

I waved away Oz's mischief and asked for two bottles of water, which swiftly arrived, along with the *cezve* pot, coffee vapour visibly curling up into the air between us. I grasped the handle and poured. Oz dropped two sugar cubes into his coffee, paused, then added a third. "Don't fucking judge me, Englishman," he said with a smile while he stirred his drink.

"Wouldn't dream of it," I said, then paused as two metallic dishes of baked eggs with vegetables descended to the table in front of us, a basket of flat bread in between.

"Enjoy," said the waitress and ducked back in between the bead curtain in the doorway.

I tore a piece of bread and dipped it into my plate, scooping out egg and a chunk of pepper. "Mmmm … oh man, this *is* good."

"I told you," Oz said, then attacked his own meal.

"So, how much are the scooters going to set us back?"

Oz shook his head, then pointed to his overfull mouth. He chewed, swallowed, took a sip of water, then grinned at me. "Not scooters, scooter. We only need one. You drive, I'll ride on back."

"Why me? You know the roads better"

"I slept three hours." He gave me the finger across the table.

I shrugged my shoulders. I didn't feel as tired as Oz looked. "Fair enough. Do you know where we're heading exactly?"

"Behind where you're sitting, the way she came into town, there are only two villages that way before the slopes of Babadag get too steep. No one lives in the higher places."

Babadag is the mountain. The tallest in Anatolia. It looms, with its little brother, over everything in the region. Wherever you are, you can see it. When the rainclouds push over the top of it, they can be on you in minutes, dumping buckets of water before you even know they've arrived. And Oz was right. No-one lived any higher than the foothills.

"Did you email the imam?" Oz asked, mopping up what was left of the tomato and yogurt sauce from his breakfast with bread.

"I did. I sincerely hope we don't need him. But I explained the situation and asked for his advice anyway." I pushed my plate away, drained the last of my coffee and wiped my mouth. I eyed the menu to see what we owed and tucked a few notes under my plate, then stood. "Now, where do we get this scooter?"

"Follow me."

***

The cobbled street of the touristy centre soon gave way to a roughly hewn dirt track. Great lumps of rock and breeze-block fragments from abandoned constructions helped me keep my wits about me as I shakily steered the scooter up the hillside.

"You're doing fine," Oz said, as if reading my thoughts.

"Don't distract me, or I'll catch one of those bricks! How far to the first village?"

I followed his finger as he pointed over my shoulder to the northwest. "See the dome?"

I picked out the shimmering blue tiles of a small mosque. "Got it. Can't be more than a couple Ks," I said and twisted the throttle. The scooter burst forward, kicking up a cloud of sand-coloured dust around us. Within minutes we were slowing to a stop a few metres from the first group of houses. I rested the bike on its stand and secured the two helmets with the chain Oz's friend at the hire shop had given us.

"You'll do the talking, right?" I asked.

Oz shook his head, trying to restore some shape to his shaggy hair and laughed. "I don't think the villagers know much English. Wait here."

I sheltered under the shade of a pomegranate tree and watched as Oz rapped on the first door and waited. When the door opened, a headscarf-toting old woman looked him up and down before even allowing him to speak. As he told his story, though, she seemed more amenable, ultimately covering her mouth and nose with her hands, as if in prayer. She reached out a hand and touched him tenderly on his shoulder, then closed the door. Oz ambled back to me, looking defeated.

"What did she say?"

"She doesn't know the widow. Says there are only three families in the village. Nobody here was widowed since her mother. She died ten years ago. Maybe more. Fuck."

"Okay, but what about the other village? How far is it?"

Oz lit a cigarette from the tin in his pocket. "Five, maybe six kilometres more." He blew smoke out in a dense cloud, then wafted it away from me. "Sorry, man. But you saw her. Her leg was … fucking bad. And she came eight kilometres? Nine?"

"No buses here? No dolmus?"

Oz shrugged. "It's *possible*. Or to come in a van. A cart."

"We should at least take a look. We have the scooter."

"We should. We should." He finished his cigarette and unfastened the helmets. "I'll drive," he said and climbed on. I took my place behind him, and we tore off, up the steeper hill path which led to the ascent of the mountain proper. Oz was steadier on the bike—unsurprising, as it's the main method of transport in the area in the summer months— and we made good time.

As we crested the first of the foothills, bringing the peak of Babadag into view, dark clouds rolled over the summit and began their breakneck tumble toward us.

"Don't worry," Oz said. "Too thin to carry much rain."

I murmured affirmatively in reply.

Fifteen minutes later, the clouds had cleared without so much as a shower, and we were outside the community hall of the bigger of the two villages. Prayers had not long finished, and children milled around a grassy area out front, while their parents and what looked like most of the other adults in the community conversed enthusiastically. I elected to join Oz as he approached three older men who were smoking.

I noticed Oz switch to Arabic as he explained the situation, reciting the increasingly familiar rhythm of those first few beats of the curse the old woman had placed upon him. A man in robes and a silk-embroidered felt hat hurried over, waving one hand, the other covering his lips in a silencing gesture. From the speed of his approach, I wondered if he was going to attack us at first, but he smiled when Oz stopped talking and reached out and embraced Oz in the customary fashion, touching the temples of each side of their heads together in turn.

"Welcome to you, also," he said and offered me his hand, which I shook.

"I'm sorry, my Turkish is not good," I said, immediately wondering if my slow, spaced-out intonation had come across as patronising.

"No problem. You are welcome."

He released my hand and immediately turned back to Oz, speaking animatedly, his tone rising as he asked questions, and reacted with what seemed like shock to the story. The small crowd of villagers surrounding us thickened until it began to feel claustrophobic. The exchange stopped abruptly and died off to silence. The imam stroked his thick, silvery beard, his eyes fixed on some far-off place on the horizon.

"Mate, what's he said?" I spoke quietly, jabbing Oz in the abdomen.

Oz raised his hand. "Wait. One moment."

The imam fixed his eyes on Oz's and uttered a short, staccato sentence. Then he turned to me. "Your friend will need you. Inshallah, you find this widow."

I thanked him, then Oz led me back to the bike, his arm tight to my shoulder.

"So, what's going on?" I said when we stopped, unfastening the helmets and handing Oz's to him.

Oz hooked his helmet around the handlebars and lit a cigarette. "He said there are no widows here, either. None like ours, anyway. But he said he saw her. In a meditation vision. He's a Sufi. It's how they pray."

"Okay …"

"He saw someone like her. With something dark. All around. And inside."

"Okay, but how does that help us? *Does* that help us?"

"Maybe it helps. When he was looking away. I told you to be quiet?"

"I remember, yeah."

"He was trying to remember the place he saw."

"And?"

"And he's not sure. Not one hundred percent. But he remembers white blocks. Around her as she slept. Where the *dark* entered. White blocks all around. Like square but … higher. I don't remember the word in English."

"Rectangular?"

"Rectangle, yes."

"Like the cemetery?"

Oz nodded. He stubbed out his cigarette on the gnarled trunk of an old olive tree and got back on the bike.

***

Cemeteries in the Muslim world are, unlike those we're used to in the west, often disconnected from religious buildings. Much like the necropolises found in Iberia, they are commonly flat, open structures. Gleaming white headstones and tombs dotted at regular intervals. The burial ground for that town was on the other side of a flood plain, to the northeast. It shone in the early afternoon sun as we took the sweeping curve around the meadow.

"Do you see it?" Oz shouted over the din of the engine.

"See wha—" I stopped short as I picked out the black veil, billowing like a flag in the breeze. "Oh. I see it. Fuck, I see it."

We pulled up at the entrance and dashed through the gate and across the cemetery toward where the veil was caught. I froze several metres away as I processed what I saw, grabbing at Oz's vest and tugging him back.

"Oz, mate. Wait. Do you realise—"

"I do." He turned to me. "I need to see."

The veil was lodged under a fractured slab of white stone. We were still too far away to tell whether it was the *same* veil the widow had been wearing, but somehow, I think we both just knew. The slab made up one-third of the cover of a grave. The other fragments were nowhere to be seen. I strode after Oz, not wanting him to face it alone. We moved in step to the edge of the grave and peered in.

A small, hunched skeleton—unclear as to whether it belonged to a child or a slight woman— lay on its side in the cavity in the ground. I turned on my flashlight app on my phone and shone it into the dark space. I traced the path of the light down the body until I found the bones of the leg, showing no signs of a fracture.

"Look at the leg. I don't think it's the same woman."

"Let's open the grave more, to be sure."

I glanced around, fearful of being watched, then, finding no one, nodded my head and began to heave away the upper part of the broken cover slab.

When I saw Oz's drawn face, his mouth a near-invisible horizontal line, I placed the heavy stone to one side and skirted the edge of the grave. I crouched beside him to see what he was staring at. The jawbone hung open in a never-ending scream, while the bone material of the skull around the eye sockets was charred to a fierce black.

# CHAPTER FOUR

"Do you really think now is the time to fuck off to Tunisia, Oz?"

Marie was not on board with our travel plans.

Once we'd photographed the skeleton in the open grave, we reported it to the local police, who in turn put up a sign outside the cemetery, warning vandals about 'damage to public property.' Neither of us supposed it was worth trying to explain what we suspected had really happened.

Once we'd emailed the photo to our man in Tunisia, he sent a flurry of replies, offering sympathy and, if we needed it, a meeting. With Sıla still in the hospital and unresponsive to stimuli, though at least stable, we did need it. So, I'd booked us both on a flight, with a flexible return date, to Tunis. Then Marie had got home from her beach yoga class.

"This isn't a holiday." Oz was yelling so fiercely, the muscles in his neck were pulled taut.

"I get that. But your niece is in a coma, for fuck's sake! What am I supposed to do? I can barely communicate with Enes."

"You don't have to be always at the hospital. Enes will understand. Tell the family we have guests at the apartment."

"And where do I tell them you are? And why?"

"I'll speak with Enes before we go." He turned to me. "The flight is tomorrow, yes?"

"Ten to seven from Dalaman to Ataturk, then on to Tunis from there."

"So, there is time." He moved closer to her and held her face in his hands. "Marie, I must do this. Maybe it's the only way to help Sila."

My phone burst to life on the table, the pounding drums of an Arch Enemy track earning me more daggers from Marie. I held up a hand in apology and dashed to answer before the thrashy guitars kicked in and made it worse. "Deniz? How are you doing?"

"Boiling hot and thirsty. Are you going to let me in?"

"What?"

"I'm in the street. Boy, are you slow."

I moved to the window. She stood outside beside a decent-sized rucksack, wearing a shirt and over-the-knee cargo shorts, her wild hair coiled into two thick braids. She grinned and waved enthusiastically.

"What are you doing?"

"Open the door, dummy."

I spun around. Oz looked perplexed, while Marie just looked even more furious.

"Did you know she was coming?"

"Not at all. I gave her the address in case she found any more materials related to the curse. And I told her about the trip, obviously."

"Obviously," said Marie, clearly bemused. Then, turning to Oz: "You didn't tell me the professor was a woman."

I opened the internal door, then turned back. "Can you guys hold the domestic for now?"

Marie bit her lip.

"Good. Thank you." I hurried down the stairs.

"Finally." Deniz handed me her rucksack. "How's Oz holding up?" she said as she passed me on the stairs.

I trudged up behind her, regretting slinging the heavy pack onto just one shoulder. "He's surviving. Concerned, naturally."

"Naturally," she said and walked through the open door. "Oz, how are you?" Oz shrugged. "And you must be Marie. Mashallah, look at you and your golden hair. I can see why this boy fell in love with you." She thrust an arm toward her.

Marie's expression noticeably softened, and she shook Deniz's hand. "Thank you," she said. "Are you going with them, then?"

"Yes, *are* you?" I said, heaving the bag onto the vacant luggage table.

"Well, I thought about it, and this is such a good opportunity for me. I can see my field in action. How often can someone like me say that?" She shot Oz a glance. "Sorry. Not treating your niece as a study project." She pulled out a chair from the small table and sat. "Not to mention that neither of you speaks Arabic. And French will only get you so far. Especially in Kairouan."

My eyes met Oz's. "Well, I guess we'll have to see if there are any seats left on the flights."

"Oh no." She dashed across the room and delved into the side pouch-pocket of her rucksack. "Already got mine." She flashed her eccentric grin at me, and I realised there was no arguing. Her reasoning also made an awful lot of sense. She would know what questions to ask when we had the audience with our cleric and perhaps pick out details we would miss.

"I need to get some things," I said. "I only brought a couple changes of clothes and my shoulder bag. Where can I get some clothing and a rucksack around here?"

"Clothes are easy," Marie said. "It's market day on the edge of town. I know the best stalls for all the genuine fakes you need. A rucksack, you might need to get a cab into the city."

"You'll come with me? To the market, I mean."

"I will if you buy lunch." Marie's mood had apparently improved in the last five minutes.

"Deal," I said and made to leave. "Oh, Deniz, what are you going to do? Do you want to come with us?"

"I should find a hotel for the night. I have the impression I'll need a good night's sleep."

"No, no. Forget that. This room has a sofa bed. I'll sleep there and you can have the bed. Unless you don't want to share with me, which I'd understand."

"A-ha. I came prepared to share with you guys. I brought my grandma pyjamas." She threw her head back, laughing. "But thanks, that would save me a lot of trouble."

"Great. Let's go shopping."

***

The following morning, Marie borrowed Oz's parents' minivan to drop us at the airport. The queue to check-in for the internal flight up to Istanbul was quiet, the plane only seating a hundred and twenty-five people and this being the earliest of three in the day. We moved toward the entrance to security.

"Look after him, or you'll have *much* worse than your bloody djinn to worry about," Marie said, then gave me a farewell hug.

I knew she was only half-joking. "I'll do my very best," I said.

She sauntered over to Oz, threw her arms around him and kissed him. "You'd better check in every day. I'll send your mother after you otherwise."

Oz blushed. "Now I'm *really* frightened. I'll miss you, aşkım. We'll be back soon."

We quickly made our way through the deserted security channel and found a group of chairs to sit and wait on.

"Right, who wants breakfast?" I stood, eyeing the cafés and restaurants lining one wall of the gate area.

"Seb, you know this is the third most expensive passenger airport in the world for cafés, right?" Deniz said, lifting her hand luggage bag from the floor.

"I … did *not* know that."

"You flew from here ten days ago, man," Oz said, laughing. "Did the French pay?"

"I was too hungover from the music bar." I looked at my watch. "Still an hour till the flight."

"What would you boys do without me, eh?" Deniz opened the flap of her small pack and pulled out a box made of thin card.

"Is that?"

"Mmhmm."

She opened the lid, revealing a full dozen plump, round pieces of baklava, syrup shimmering around the green sea of crushed pistachios. I reached out to take one.

"Uh-uh," she said, pulling the box back. "I thought to bring something. You guys can get the coffee."

"Fair enough," I said.

Oz stood and stuffed his hand into his rear pocket. "Don't know how much money I have."

"I'll get this. Come on." I led the way across the gate area to the only open café offering Turkish coffee and ordered.

"You think it's possible to help Sıla? You think this imam knows something that can help us?" Oz was agitated. He'd been quiet since the night before. At the market, at lunch, and at the apartment when we'd got back. I supposed it was good that this worry was finally coming out.

"I'd say 'think' is too strong a word. But if Deniz says he's the best we can do without going to Mecca—and I literally *can't* go to Mecca—then I think he's worth a shot. And look how quickly he came back to us after he saw the grave. He *wants* to help us. Which is half the battle." I laid a note on the counter, took the three coffees on a tray and began to amble back across to where Deniz sat with our bags.

"How is Kairouan?" Oz said, his curiosity now uncorked.

"I don't follow. What do you mean?"

"What's it like? You went before, yes?"

"Ah, okay. Well, yes. I went there once before, in 2010. On a leisure trip. I was in Tunis for work, some new finds had been brought in to the Bardo Museum from a dig outside Carthage, including some pots and tablets that turned out to be Hittite."

Oz mimed sleep, even making snoring sounds.

"Alright. Message received. I'll get to the point. So, I went down there via El Djem—the place with the amphitheatre from the Gladiator film—and Sousse, which is a ghastly little tourist town now, with only a few pockets that retain any authenticity."

Oz threw his head back and laughed. "This is getting to the point?"

"Context is *everything*, Oz. And piss off." I smiled at him, to make sure he understood I was kidding. "Anyway, I went down on the Louage. It's a bus, a bit like your Dolmuş, but they use cars—station wagons—instead of a van. And they don't leave until they're full. I remember leaving Sousse at half eight in the morning and it was chilly, for north Africa. Fifteen degrees, something like that. When we arrived in Kairouan, forty minutes later, guess the local temperature." I paused.

"No idea. Twenty-five."

"Thirty-nine."

"Fuck."

"Yeah, exactly, mate. Do you know what Napoleon's generals supposedly called Kairouan when they took it in 1881?"

Oz shook his head.

"The holy city in hell."

He laughed again. "Don't tell the imam."

"Yes, don't," said Deniz, rising to take her coffee from the tray. "When were you there?"

"2010. I was just telling Oz about it."

"Boring." Oz whispered the word just loudly enough for me to hear.

I shot him faux daggers.

"Before the Arab Spring. I think it will be … trickier for us this time." Deniz said.

"How so?" I sat, reaching over and taking a gooey piece of baklava with a napkin.

"You probably heard about the Salafists and the Uqba Bin Nafi groups there. The government has them more or less under control in the capital and the tourism zones. But the holy city. Most governments still advise against foreigners travelling there."

Oz took a couple of pieces of baklava, stuffing one directly into his mouth. "Mmmm … Sorry. Mmmm … Is it dangerous? For us?"

"For us? I suppose not. For our friend? Perhaps." Deniz nodded in my direction.

"Thanks for that," I said.

The Turkish Airlines attendant at the desk in front of us read out our flight number over the public address. We looked around. The place was still almost deserted. The early charters and low-cost flights hadn't ramped up the schedules this early in the summer. We scoffed down a little more of our breakfast, downed our coffees and stepped forward for boarding.

Conditions were perfect for flying. I gazed down at the scenery as it grew ever more distant during our ascent, the morning sun glinting off the Aegean Sea, as the islands that dotted the Anatolian coast were reduced to no more than specks amid the sparkling waves. I rested my eyes once we reached cruising altitude, until the attendants brought along our breakfast of omelettes with *sucuk* sausages and Turkish tea. By the time we'd finished eating, we were already beginning our descent into Ataturk International, the sea narrowing into the strait of the Bosphorus.

It was only as the plane banked steeply over the three grand mosques of Sultanahmet that I realised none of us had spoken since we'd boarded. It could have been tiredness—it was still before eighty thirty—but a look at Deniz and Oz's tightly-drawn expressions told me it was more likely the apprehension that made my chest tight too.

Once we'd filtered through the airport's transfer channel, we found ourselves in departures, with a bit more than an hour until our connection onward to Tunis. Oz hopped from one foot to another, gazing around the terminal at the neon signs above the various shops and restaurants.

"I'm going to get a second breakfast," he said confidently.

"Isn't that third, technically?" Deniz raised an eyebrow as she spoke.

"Baklava doesn't count" He winked, before moseying off toward a place offering toasted wraps. I gestured to a bank of empty seats and we sat, piling our hand luggage onto the small table to one side.

"Sure you don't want a coffee or anything?" I said, eyeing the cafés immediately in front of us.

"Too much caffeine makes me jittery," she said, stretching her legs out in front of her. "How long have you known Oz?"

I laughed. "Actually, in total, only about eight months. Spread out over the past three summers. He's been my landlord while I was in the area for a translation job. We've become pretty close, though."

"Must have done, to be doing all this. Kairouan will be … risky. For *you* especially, in the current climate."

"He's a good man. And without contacts …"

"Like me?" Her mouth contorted into her habitual, over-the-top grin.

"Like you, yes. Without that, how would he deal with something like this?"

"You're a believer now, then?" Her smile erased itself from her face and she looked intently into my eyes.

I thought about it for a moment. "I think *believer* is a very strong word. But what we saw in the graveyard, what the imam told us—the Sufi guy in the mountain village, I mean—then what *you* said. About the practicality of mutilating all those goats. Who *could* do that, let alone finding the time and—"

"'Yes' would have been enough." Her smug expression was restored.

"Let me ask *you* something," I said, after a pause.

"Anything. I am an open book." She opened her arms exaggeratedly, as though playing charades with a simpleton.

"What made you go to the states to study? Must've been expensive."

"I actually won a scholarship, so *they* paid *me*. Or my university here did. It's a complex set-up. Anyway, I was doing Middle Eastern studies—history, literature, a bit of language—hence the Arabic. And I thought, 'what would the perspective on this material be like from the outside?' When I saw the program, I worked my butt off, got accepted and went there for the first year of my master's."

"Wow, impressive. And how'd you find it?"

"Welcoming. I was on the west coast, Seattle. And the president wasn't a paranoid psychotic with a reading age of eleven."

I almost choked.

"But perspective-wise, I found a reasonable amount of suspicion, and fairly complicated agendas. Pro-Saudi. Anti-Iran. I guess it was what I expected. But it's all tied up in oil and money. Everything in this part of the world is, I guess." I couldn't disagree.

Oz strolled back over, clutching a foil-wrapped flatbread. "This thing is *great*," he said and took another huge bite.

"What's in it?" I said, feeling no hunger whatsoever.

"Cheese, spinach, some seeds. They make it quick, and it isn't that expensive. Want me to—"

"I'm good."

Oz sat between us and finished his wrap. He took out a water bottle from his backpack and glugged some of it down.

"Look," I said, sometime later, pointing to the screen. "Our flight's boarding. Gate eleven. Let's go."

The flight was far busier than the early morning shuttle up from Dalaman. Mainly business travellers, by the looks of it. We were crammed into a bank of three, Oz taking the window this time, while Deniz took the middle and I sat in the aisle. We were airborne more or less on time, expecting to land in Tunis around noon, the time zone a couple hours behind Istanbul.

"What's the plan when we get to Tunis? Will we travel south immediately?" Deniz asked.

Oz pried his nose away from the window to tune in.

"Well, it's up to you both, to be honest," I said. "I contacted my mate at the Bardo—the guy who gave me that Hittite job I mentioned—and told him we would be in the country. He said he'd be happy to help us. Might even have somewhere we can stay. Closer to Kairouan."

"Some local knowledge would definitely be a help. We're meeting our cleric on Thursday, right?"

"Exactly."

"Two days to get down there. I think it makes sense. What do you say, Oz?"

Oz stroked the straggly stubble on his chin. "I'm so tired. Marie said it's not a holiday. But I haven't slept well since that first day with the widow. For me, meeting your friend is okay."

"It's settled then. When we land, I'll give him a call and see when he's available. I know a decent place in the city centre, near the main railway station, which is clean and cheap."

"They have breakfast?" Oz's priorities were ever clear.

"Excellent breakfast. Even make their own fig jam, if I remember correctly."

"Nice."

"Speaking of food …" I eyed the flight attendants wheeling their trolley down the aisle from the front. "Who's ready for lunch?"

Deniz covered her mouth. "I feel like I've barely digested my breakfast."

The meal wasn't too enormous, and we found our hunger from somewhere. I gratefully accepted a glass of white wine as accompaniment to my *mezze*, then read back over some of the documents Deniz had sent me after our initial meeting. Deniz dozed, while Oz had his nose glued to the window, this being only his sixth flight in his life, the others being between Dalaman and the capital and the one time he'd visited Marie's family in Kent.

"Look, Seb!" he called out some time after the plane had begun its descent.

The Cap Bon peninsula extended like an arid finger, beckoning us toward our destination.

"Beautiful," he said.

"It is. See the fort?" I pointed to the sandstone building on the opposite side of the peninsula's ridge.

"Mmm."

"The view across the water from there is breathtaking. There's an island that belongs to Italy … But we won't have time. Sorry, mate. I need to stay focussed on what we're here for."

"It's okay. I understand. I see you love this place."

"I really do."

"More than *Turkiye?*"

I feigned considering it. "Nah. Course not."

The seatbelt sign illuminated, and the attendants announced that my laptop needed to go away. I put it into sleep mode and stashed it above my head, then prepared for landing.

Deniz stirred to life. "Are we there already?" she asked, yawning and stretching.

"Landing, yep."

We zoomed over the grimy, off-white, low-rise apartments that surrounded the airport and touched down with barely a bump. A few minutes later we were descending the stairs onto the tarmac to wait for the bus to the terminal. The sun was searing, the heat drier here than back in Turkey. "Even you must be feeling it here," I said, turning to Oz.

He stood in a singular spot of shadow.

Acres of concrete and dozens of aircraft were bathed in bright sunlight, heat haze rising whichever way you looked. And there stood Oz, in his own personal patch of shade. His head darted one way then the other.

"Oh, mate. This is just your luck lately. Come stand over here," I said, beckoning.

"This has *nothing* to do with luck, Seb. Look!" Deniz pointed to the cloud blocking the sun from where Oz stood. It was an impenetrable black, in a clear animal shape, feline with pointed ears and a short tail curved behind the body.

"Looks like a cat," I said.

"Close. A hyena. The most common form the ghul take when they appear independently of a host, according to the scripture. Step away, Oz. Come to me." Oz stepped forward, Deniz taking his arm and pulling him to stand beside her. "Do you feel strange? Lightheaded?"

Oz shook his head. "I feel … normal." A single drop of blood crept from his nose and down his chin before his legs turned to jelly and he almost collapsed.

Deniz and I both stepped forward, steadying him, before sharing a glance which said everything about our concerns.

The bus pulled up behind us, its hydraulics noisily announcing the doors opening. We turned and boarded, Deniz and I guiding Oz, clearly shaken, despite his saying otherwise. I leaned across to the window and looked up to see the patch of cloud disperse to nothing.

# Chapter Five

"Seb, grab the bags. I'm going to find somewhere to sit Oz down," Deniz said as we stepped off the bus and into the arrivals building.

Without hesitation, I dashed over to the carousel. I cast my eyes over to them between scouring the many cases and holdalls rotating in front of me on the conveyor until I spotted the first bag—Deniz's—and heaved it over to where they waited.

"How you doing, mate?" I said as I placed it on the floor in front of them.

Oz's eyes were angled toward mine, but unfocused, distant. "I'm okay, man. Just … dizzy."

The trail of blood from his nose had been wiped away.

"I'm going to grab the other baggage. I'll call my contact at the Bardo, too. He knows we're here, but we've not made any arrangements yet. If you need me—"

"You'll know about it," said Deniz, forcing a smile.

As the kaleidoscope of bags whirred by, I dug through my contact list and called Ibrahim. It was a tonic to hear a friendly voice on the other end of the phone, one untouched by all this madness. Within two minutes, we had an open invitation to a much better place than the hotel.

Oz was on his feet when I lugged the remaining two bags over. I placed them in a pile with Deniz's.

"Are you sure you're okay to carry on?" I asked.

Oz nodded his head. His eyes remained distant, but at least were able to hold my gaze.

"What do you reckon?" I said, turning to Deniz.

"He's steady on his feet, so I think we should get to the hotel. Give him a chance to lie down."

"We're going to skip the hotel. Head straight to the museum. Ibrahim said he's got more than enough room for all of us at his house up at Sidi Bou Said, just out of town. Wouldn't take no for an answer."

"What about breakfast? Fig jam?" Oz's face scrunched into an expression somewhere between shock and disgust.

"Looks like somebody's feeling more like their old self." I winked at Deniz, and we guided Oz through passport control and customs to the taxi pick up.

We hopped into an old Peugeot estate, the youngish driver all smiles as he helped pile our bags into the boot. "La Musée Bardo, s'il vous plait," I said, taking my seat.

"Oui, bien sûr," said the driver and sped off. "Français?" he asked, grinning.

"Anglais," I said, taking in the busy city scenery as we moved onto Boulevard Bouazizi, the newly resurfaced dual carriageway that sliced through the heart of the city. Scores of whitewashed apartment buildings flashed by, occasionally interrupted by rectangular minarets and grand monuments from the days of the dictatorship.

"English! Lovely jubbly!"

I grimaced. "Yes. Something like that."

"Your friends? Your wife? Not English?" he said, eyes on the rearview mirror, as he swerved around heavily laden produce trucks.

Deniz leaned forward and said something sharp in Arabic. The taxi driver burst into a fit of laughter.

"What did you say?" I said, looking back.

"I said we're Turkish. And that you should be so lucky to have me as a wife."

"Ouch." I faced front as we veered onto the exit ramp and down to street level, just a few turns from the Bardo. I dug into my pocket for my wallet and pulled out enough cash for the price on the meter and a decent tip. "*Merci, monsieur,*" I said and stepped out of the car.

I slung my bag on my back and placed my hands on Oz's shoulders. "Feeling okay?"

He smiled. "Better. A lot. Sorry for before."

"Nothing to apologise for. Just glad you're alright," I said, and led the way across the road to the museum entrance. The pure white façade of the entrance bore no scars of 2015's horrendous terrorist attack, having long since been replastered and painted. So much had happened since the last time I'd been in the country.

I led the others up to the security gates and called over one of the guards. "I'm here to see Dr. Ibrahim Gharbi. He's expecting me. It's Seb Mackie."

"Wait here, please." The man scuttled off behind the reception desk and through a door at the rear.

"Can we look around the museum?" Oz was staring at the shiny, new-looking screens on the far wall that phased between elaborate mosaics, ancient pottery and medieval Arabic glassware.

"I think we should talk to Ibrahim first," I said. "It's an amazing collection though. I can show you those Hittite tablets I mentioned earli—"

Oz held his hands together, pleadingly. "Forget I asked." He smiled. "I joke with you. Just a joke. I want to see it."

"I'd like to look at the collection, too. Especially some of the scriptural originals and mosque lamps."

"I'll ask Ibrahim, see what he can do."

"Ask me what?" A familiar, gravelly voice bellowed from behind me. I turned and embraced the man walking toward me in the white, mandarin-collared suit. "How are you, Seb, my boy. You look just the same as you did nearly a decade ago. I know I don't. I've got fat. That's marriage, and

Emine's cooking." He belly-laughed, his eyes almost disappearing behind rounded cheeks.

I stepped back. "This is Professor Deniz Yilmaz from Istanbul, and this is Oz, my friend."

Ibrahim stepped forward, shaking each of them by the hand enthusiastically. "Lovely to meet you both. If only it could be under better circumstances."

"The museum looks wonderful. I knew it before, by reputation, of course," Deniz said. "I would love to take a look around, if there's time."

"Well, I hope Seb has told you, I invite you all to stay with me and Emine. My kids have all grown up and left, so we have the space."

"You're very kind, thank you." Oz bowed his head forward as he spoke.

"It's settled then. I have some work to do here, still, and I'm waiting for a call—I may be able to arrange lodgings for you further south for tomorrow, before you make the trip to Kairouan on Thursday morning. Why don't you all take a look around the museum and I'll be done here in about an hour or so."

We all murmured our agreement. Ibrahim turned to the security guard and spoke in rapid-fire, pointed Arabic. The man hurried over and took Deniz's rucksack, leading me and Oz to the storage room where we could leave our things.

"See you in a bit," I said, and we walked into the museum.

***

I was pleasantly surprised when Oz took a real interest in the Hittite tablets I'd assisted with the translations for, while Deniz went off to the scripture collection to see some rare pieces. After that we strolled, awe-struck, around the mosaic collection for half an hour. I'd seen them all before, but two-thousand-year-old artwork, the coloured tiles fully restored to display their original vivid brightness, is something that never ceases to amaze.

We left the final mosaic room and were met with signs. One way pointed toward medieval pottery, the other to Roman-era curse tablets. "Maybe not, eh?" I said, gesturing to the sign.

Oz smiled. "Why not? Roman curses will be funny compared to mine."

"Fair point. Come on then, I'll translate."

We wandered into the narrow hallway which housed the curses.

"Shit, man. Look at this one," I said, dragging Oz to the second curse tablet. "'May worms, cancer and maggots penetrate every morsel of your body.' I wonder what he did to her?"

"Adultery. It says at the bottom of the sign."

"Ha! Well spotted. Let's look at the next. Jeez, 'let the gods kill all the horses of the green-and-white team when the next race begins.' Not very sporting of them, is it?"

"My father said worse about players from Fenerbahçe."

I chuckled. "I can believe that." We strolled along to an ornate tablet with an engraved illustration. "'May he who stole my woman'—can you *steal* a woman? Anyway, 'may he become ... liquid as water.' Yuck. What a way to go."

"Imagine though. If it worked." Oz laughed to himself, making squelching noises as he mimed turning into liquid.

"Children, quiet please. This is a museum, you know?" Deniz stood at the door, her playful smile taking up half of her face. "What are you looking at?"

"Curses," said Oz, standing up straight.

"Just can't get enough, can you? Where are they from?"

"They're Roman," I said. "Pretty hilarious, to be honest. We came in for a bit of light relief."

"What's the Arabic one over there?"

"No, no, these are all—" The words died in my mouth. There was a strip of what looked like papyrus or possibly vellum, dyed a deep, indigo blue. In bright, off-white ink, the unmistakable calligraphy of Arabic script meandered its way across the page from right to left.

Deniz dashed over and fixed her eyes on the text, her fingers absent-mindedly twizzling her long curls. "Oz. Come here." She beckoned with her free hand, without shifting her eyes from the words.

"What is it?" I followed Oz over to the corner and glared at the inscrutable text. "Guys, what is it?" I repeated myself, more forcefully this time.

"Wait a moment. Almost … Fucking hell. Excuse my language, but this is it, Oz. This is your curse."

"What?" Oz leaned forward. "Read it to me."

"I'm not reading *this* aloud."

"Yeah, perhaps *not* the best idea," I said.

"Okay, but what does it say?"

"Let me give you the edited highlights. The scorched eyes are mentioned, as are the animal entrails, which, it says, are 'to sustain the infernal hunger of the rotten one.'"

"Oh my God," I said.

"Precisely. But this is the bit. It talks about being carried by 'the wretched one'. Someone who already passed but has not found rest. Then about the soul of the young being held captive until … then it ends."

"Then it ends? Are you fucking kidding me?"

"I can't believe this." Oz paced the room, one hand covering his mouth.

"Is there information on the provenance of the piece? Any clue as to where we might find the rest?" I said, tracing my finger across the information panel. "Shit, nothing."

"What's all the commotion? Seb, is everything okay?" Ibrahim stood in the doorway with his laptop bag and a newspaper.

"Do you have the details of where this stuff came from?"

"I do, but why are you so interested in Roman curses? I thought Oz's problem was—"

"This one *isn't* Roman. It's Arabic. And much of the wording is lifted from whatever that old widow spouted at Oz," Deniz said.

"One of you take a photo of the plaque. Make sure the item code is clear. I can check the catalogue from home. Bilel, my driver, is waiting downstairs. Let's get back to my place and we can see where it's from with a G&T. Or orange juice," he said, nodding his head toward Deniz.

"Please, gin me," she said as she aimed her phone's camera. "I've got the photo. Let's go."

# Chapter Six

Bilel was a fearless driver. I suppose not many of the other drivers on the motorway tracing the southern perimeter of the airport and out toward our destination had an AMG Mercedes CLA 350. He weaved in and out of traffic, over and undertaking clapped-out old Peugeots, Renaults and heavily laden Daihatsu minivans. I held onto the handle above my door, taking some misguided comfort in it.

"You feeling okay, Seb? Want me to ask Bilel to slow down?" Ibrahim grinned at me, twisting around from the front seat.

Bilel eyed me in the rear-view mirror, a smirk drawn across his face.

"No. No, I'm fine. Really," I said, trying to relax my grimacing facial muscles, but continuing to clutch the handle.

Deniz and Oz gazed calmly out of the window across the shimmering water of the lake of Tunis and onto the La Goulette port, as ever a hub of cargo ships, with the occasional ferry or small cruise liner dotted between them.

A few moments later, Bilel mercifully slowed to turn off the motorway and onto the steep road uphill, toward the site of ancient Carthage.

"The place from the museum?" said Oz, catching sight of the sign.

"That's right," said Ibrahim. "The seat of Hannibal and Hamilcar before him. When Tunisia was one of the centres of power of the Mediterranean."

We skirted around Byrsa Hill and its ruins, then began to descend once more to the charming village streets of Sidi Bou Said. Small houses were packed together like sardines, their simple whitewashed stone walls opening up into the famously ornate blue, wooden doors, decorated with spirals and curves of wrought iron. Bright bougainvillea contrasted with the azure of the wood.

"Mashallah! You live here?" Deniz asked, no small amount of awe in her voice.

"Not quite. Just on the other side of that small hill. But we have a deck and a pool." Ibrahim beamed with pride. The car zoomed up the rise and down the other side. We slowed to a stop and Bilel hit a button on his remote. The wide double gate crept open and he drove in, pulling up on the drive.

Ibrahim said something to him in Arabic and he quickly rounded the car, pulling the three rucksacks from the rear and gesturing for us to follow him into the house. Oz and I heaved our bags onto our backs, while he disappeared off ahead with Deniz's slung over his shoulder.

"See you out the back in a few moments. I'll prepare some drinks," Ibrahim called after us.

The house was set out on a single floor, the stone pathway cutting through an immaculate lawn dotted with sprinklers. Bilel shoved open the cerulean door and kicked off his shoes, stuffing his feet into some slippers. "Chaussons," he said, pointing to a rack with more of them. We all followed suit.

He led us through a sprawling lounge whose windows looked out onto the front lawn, with a hatch through to the kitchen on the other side. "Salle de bain," he said, gesturing to what looked to be the communal bathroom. He stopped outside a pair of doors, just beyond and gestured. "Madame ici. Messieurs là-bas."

"Merci," I said.

"Shukran," Deniz added.

Bilel gave us a swift nod and hurried out, the sound of his motorcycle starting up and speeding off following rapidly. Oz and I ditched our packs in our room before I led him and Deniz out into the back garden. Emine was putting ice cubes and lemon slices into glasses at one end of the garden table, while Ibrahim, now in a loose fitting short-sleeved shirt and shorts, was firing up his laptop at the other.

"These chairs are useless," he said. "You can't get them close enough to the table."

"Sure it's not just your belly?" Emine asked, smiling wickedly. She came over and greeted us warmly.

Emine was a visual artist, working in sculpture and other three-dimensional media mainly. Almost a decade younger than Ibrahim, they'd met a couple years after the end of Ibrahim's first marriage and had married after a whirlwind six months. This was the first time I'd met her, but it was easy to see the warmth between them.

"Okay then, I'm in the catalogue. Professor, do you have that photograph?" said Ibrahim.

"Deniz, please. I feel weird even when the students call me professor. Here."

She handed over the phone and Ibrahim carefully tapped in the nine-digit code on the plaque beside it.

He waited. "Not found. Hmmm. Let me double check it." He tapped away once more, holding the phone next to the laptop screen and whispering the sequence in Arabic as he checked. He tapped enter and waited. "Still not found. Maybe it's listed under the name."

He continued the search, entering three different combinations of the title of the piece from the plaque, each time coming up with no results. He cursed under his breath as Emine handed glasses to each of us and gestured for us to sit at the table.

"This doesn't make any sense at all!" Ibrahim thumped the table and took a long swig of his drink. "How can it be there if it's not in the damned catalogue?"

We all remained quiet.

"Why don't you check with Midou? Doesn't he populate the catalogue?" Emine said, finally.

Ibrahim's eyes darted upwards as he thought about it. "I'll get my phone," he said and shoved his chair back, the legs grinding noisily on the patio tiles. He stalked into the house, his movements stiff, agitated. As he came back, he was yelling into the phone in Arabic, cheeks flushed purple.

"Sorry," he said, sitting. "Really. I don't usually lose my temper like that."

Emine moved her chair closer and placed her hand over his. "What did Midou say?"

"He said there's nothing later than third century in that corridor. Nothing that isn't Roman and that the clue should be in the sign above your head as you enter."

"But what about the photo?" Deniz placed her drink down and grabbed hold of her phone.

"What indeed? *That's* what I told him." He took off his glasses and cleaned them with a cloth from his pocket. "I'm sorry. I'm getting riled up again. Midou said he'll go into the museum early in the morning, before you guys set off, to clarify things. Now, shall we eat?"

"Not to put any pressure on you, Emine, but Ibrahim has been talking up your culinary skills," I said.

"Oh really? Well, tonight, I can't take any of the credit. He spent two hours last night marinating the lamb and charring vegetables for tonight's dinner."

I spun to look at my blushing friend. "Man, I didn't know you had it in you."

"It's been so long. And I thought you fellows needed a good send off before heading south. Come and help me take it out of the oven, would you?"

I followed Ibrahim into the kitchen. He opened the door of the oven and the rich fragrance of spiced meat wafted out, setting my stomach grumbling.

"Can you grab the mechouia from the fridge?" he said, nodding while he eased the roasting dish out and set it down on the counter.

"Shall I take it straight to the table?"

"Not yet, Seb. Put it down for a moment. I wanted to warn you about something. Have a seat. This won't take a minute." Ibrahim's face was grave, its lines somehow deeper than they'd been moments earlier. I lowered myself into a seat at the small table.

"Go on. I'm ready."

"First of all, let me give you these." He handed over a paper wallet with the SNCFT logo on the front. "First class train tickets to Sousse for the three of you. There's a key in there, along with a security card, too. My sister has said you can stay in their summer house on the edge of town. It's one of the new condos on the road between the old town and that dreadful resort at Kantaoui."

"Ibrahim, seriously. Thank you so much. I still don't know why I had to sit down, though."

"Yes, well that's for what I'm about to tell you now." He strode over and took the seat opposite mine. "Since the Arab Spring, you may have seen that we've had … problems with Salafists. The attack on the Bardo was terrible. Terrible for footfall, but for the wider nation too. Then when the beach shooting happened in Sousse …"

"I read about it, obviously. But we'll be careful. And the government has it under control now, no?"

"Did you go out to Kairouan when you were here working with me? I can't remember."

"I did, yes. But I was only here ten days, it was in and out. A quick look around the graveyard and the mosque and back on the louage. There wasn't really enough time to see it properly."

"You'll remember, the road there from Sousse cuts through a lot of nothing. Desert. Scrubland. Mostly abandoned. You can imagine, with the holy city there, the militant groups have chosen that as their battleground. And with government advice to tourists against travelling there, it's not well policed. It's not safe, Seb. Not even for me. And certainly not for outsiders."

"What do you suggest? Hire our own car?"

"God no! You'll be carjacked and that'll be the end of that. I'm saying if you *must* go, then take the louage, keep your head down and let your friends do the talking. But what I'm *really* saying, as your friend, is that you shouldn't go. Please, don't go."

"Ibrahim, come on. I'll be careful, but I'm not just going to leave them to it."

"Deniz is an expert in the field. She'll ask the right questions. Oz will understand. He won't want to put you at risk. Seb, my friend, I wouldn't be saying this if I didn't really believe you might be in danger." He placed his hand on mine and squeezed. He forced his features into a smile, but the concern was written large across his face.

"That lamb's going to be getting cold. We should—"

"Right, yes. Take that salad, lead on." He nudged my elbow and carefully lifted the ceramic tray with the lamb in it. "Sorry, Seb. For worrying."

"You're a good friend, Ibrahim," I said. "Thank you for worrying, really."

Walking out from the cool of the shady kitchen into the heat of the garden was striking, sweat beading on my forehead and beneath my shirt.

"Ah, they didn't get lost after all," Deniz said, and began making space at the centre of the table for the dishes.

"Wow." Oz licked his lips. "The lamb smells too good. What's the mush?"

"That's the mechouia salad. My mama's recipe," Ibrahim said, planting a spoon into the green paste. "Charred carrots, onions, tomatoes, peppers, blended with a little oil. It's huge here in Tunisia. But a little spicy, be careful." He winked and offered the spoon to Oz, who took a generous portion and passed it across to Deniz. He scooped a little with a torn piece of flatbread.

"Delicious," he said, before moving his plate over to Emine, who heaped slices of spiced lamb onto it.

"Guys, Ibrahim's sister has left us the keys to her condo on the outskirts of Sousse, so we don't need to find accommodation," I said.

"That's the tourist shithole without culture?" said Oz, between bites.

"Erm … well …"

Ibrahim belly laughed. "You've prepared them well, Seb. It is. It's sad, but it's true. But the condo is comfortable and convenient for the louage station to Kairouan."

"Thank you again," said Deniz.

"Oh, it's nothing, really. And Seb, remember this?" Ibrahim was holding a bottle of red wine.

"Is that from—?"

"Yes. Beja. The same stuff you tried at the vineyard when we drove up there."

"How did you?"

"I have my sources."

We ate, drank, and talked into the night. About our families, about work, holidays, and about everything except the djinn and the curse. I think every one of us—even Oz—managed to forget about what might be waiting for us on the road south.

The others had just turned in, and I was ready to join them, when Ibrahim shuffled to the kitchen and came out with tumblers and a bottle.

"Boukha, but the good stuff," he said, pouring a couple fingers into each glass. Boukha is fig brandy. The only one I'd tried last time was like a cross between fig candy and petrol. I took a sip.

"Wow, this *is* the good stuff." We touched our glasses together and drank in silence, looking up at the stars.

"Do you believe in it, Seb?" Ibrahim asked.

"The djinn?"

"Mmm."

"I still don't know. But Oz does. And something strange is *definitely* going on."

"My dad was a non-believer. Most of his life. He was a philosophy professor. Philosopher in his own right, too. His books are in there somewhere." Ibrahim gestured with slightly inebriated hands. "Then, one day, he went into a lycée to give a talk to the students before they went to university. What to expect from a philosophy degree, all that, you know?"

"Okay …"

"In the middle, he just stopped. Froze there at the lectern. Then he started to tremble. Then *really* shake. He collapsed."

"Fucking hell."

"Yes, quite. Anyway, they sent the ambulance and all, you know? Checked him over and he was *completely* fine. No heart attack, stroke, what have you. But they sat him up, once he'd come round and the kids … they're all gasping. Hands over their mouths."

"What was the matter?"

"His hair had gone white. His hair wasn't like this thinning mess." Ibrahim rubbed the top of his head. "No, my dad's hair was this thick shock of jet black, even then. And then like that—in an instant—white as a dove."

"Did they ever figure out why?"

"Medically, no. But I asked my dad—of course I was outside London at boarding school at the time—but I asked him, on the phone, you know? 'What happened?' He said: 'a five-foot raven stood at the back of the room, fixed its eyes on me and was draining my life.'"

"Christ. Do you think he imagined it?"

"My dad was a bit eccentric sometimes. But he never lost that sharpness of mind. So, I don't think he did, no. Do you know what he said it was?"

I shook my head, drained what was left in my glass and placed it down on the table.

"The embodiment of a djinn." Ibrahim, too, finished his drink. "I challenged him. 'Papa, you said you didn't believe all that.' And he said down the phone: 'maybe I don't believe in God, but there are things in this world we don't understand, and I pray to whatever good there is among those things, that you never live to see what I did today.'" Ibrahim stood and stretched. "What I'm saying is, neither of us believe. Not really. But you said yourself, something is going on. Keep your eyes open and pray that whatever it is doesn't come for you." He placed his arm around my shoulder, clutching the bottle of boukha in the other. "Good night, my friend."

# Chapter Seven

"Seb," Ibrahim whispered through the door, which was open no more than a crack.

I stirred, glanced over at Oz—still fast asleep—then at my watch. Ten to seven. I brought my index finger to my lip, shushing him, and climbed out of bed, pulling on a T-shirt and following my friend out to the kitchen.

"Coffee?" he said, gesturing toward the pot on the stove, wisps of fragrant steam billowing from the spot.

"Not yet. I might lie down for a bit before we have to head out. What's up?"

"Midou called from the museum."

"And?"

"And he doesn't recognise the curse fabric. Can't match it to any inventory lists, or deliveries. Nothing."

"I had a feeling that was going to be the case, last night," Deniz said, stumbling into the kitchen in a long T-shirt, her dark curls a wild bird's nest around her head. "Is there enough coffee for me?"

"Of course." Ibrahim pottered over, poured some into a cup. "Milk? Cream? Sugar?"

"Black is fine, thank you."

"Sod it, I will have one," I said, sitting at the dining table.

"Did you both sleep well? You weren't too uncomfortable?"

"Better than most conference hotels," Deniz said, taking her coffee and drinking half of it straight down. "But anyway, back to the curse. Is there any way the provenance can be identified without documentation? Or even estimated?"

"Midou has a few ideas. But we'll need time. I'll have to call you during your journey. Sorry."

"Not your fault," I said. "We've a couple hours before we need to call the taxi."

"No need. Bilel is giving you a ride."

"Ibrahim, you've done enough—"

"I can't change it now. He'll be on his way shortly—he lives on the other side of the city."

"I owe you a very good dinner, one of these days."

"It's my pleasure, really. Now, do you want to wake Oz? Emine has gone off to her studio, but she put a couple baguettes in the oven and told me to offer you some of her fig jam. He was talking about it with her last night."

***

I was apprehensive as Bilel handed us our bags and waved us off. The train station had been the beginning for every journey I'd taken in the country almost a decade earlier. I'd felt genuine emotional pain when I'd heard of it being burnt during the Arab Spring protests in 2011. We walked across the leafy square in front of the building, and I was relieved to see the same old façade staring back at me. You could make out the charring under the renovated paintwork but, importantly, it was essentially the same place.

The air was cool as I led the others into the shade of the main concourse to find the platform for our train—the all-day express that snaked its way down the coast to Gabes, before jutting inland toward the Sahara proper and terminating at Tozeur. We would be onboard for just a couple hours.

"Platform two, guys," I said. "We've got just over ten minutes. Anyone want anything?"

Oz shrugged his shoulders. In one hand, he carried a paper bag with a fresh baguette and a small jar of jam that Ibrahim had sent him away with.

"I might get some coffee," Deniz said. "Want one?"

"Can you grab me an Arabic coffee? With cardamom."

"Sure. Be right back."

"How are you getting on?" I turned to Oz, really looked at him for the first time since the airport. He looked more rested, his eyes less bloodshot, which was a relief. "Did you speak to Marie last night?"

"She phoned, yes."

"And?"

"And she's okay. Working. Now we have guests in one of the apartments."

"What about Sıla?"

He drew in a long breath. "The same."

"Have the doctors—"

"Nothing, Seb. Now, only *we* can help, I think."

"This cleric will know what to do."

"I hope."

"He *must.*"

"One cardamom coffee," Deniz said, handing me a paper cup. "Shall we?"

We headed through the gate and over to the train, climbing the steps up into the carriage. First class was air-conditioned and even advertised Wi-Fi. I had my doubts about that, but it was definitely a different level of comfort to what I'd experienced on my last visit.

The train eased out of the station on time, rolling slowly through various quarters of the city, before heading into the surprisingly lush countryside. Oz picked at his bread and jam across from me, while Deniz and I sipped our coffee and watched the coastline whizz by to our left.

The train ride passed without incident. On arrival at Sousse station, flanked by a handful of sun worshippers, we made our way through heat that hung heavy in the air to the front of the taxi queue. I gave the first driver the paper with the address for Ibrahim's sister's apartment and we were on our way.

The majority of the three or four kilometres of the journey were along immaculately tended boulevards, lined with palm trees. It was easy to see that this was the zone for foreign tourists and the rich, a stark contrast from the more functional apartments of the city centre. We arrived at the gate to the condominium complex and the driver asked for my access card. I patted down my pockets before finding it in the envelope with the train tickets. He scanned us in and rolled the car into the underground car park.

I paid and swiped the taxi out, then inspected the key to see which unit was ours. "402, guys. Fourth floor," I said, gesturing toward the elevator in front of me. Once we'd ascended, I stuffed the key into the lock and opened the door onto a huge, minimalist space, walls in white, flooring and furnishings in a soft beige. The kitchen opened onto the lounge, with doors off to the sides for the three bedrooms and bathroom. In front was a crescent-shaped balcony which overlooked the pool, with a view to a golf course to the right and the marina to the left. It was positively palatial.

"I wish we were here for a holiday instead of … you know." Deniz laid her bag down and tested one of the sofas for comfort.

"I know." I placed my pack on the luggage rack near the door.

"Sorry, guys," said Oz and walked out to the balcony.

"Hey, Oz, no. No, no, I didn't mean it like that," Deniz said, following him.

I decided not to join them, instead melting into my chair and watching as Oz shook and Deniz comforted him. He and I were close, even after a relatively short time, but I didn't think he'd allow himself to sob like that in my arms. Call it a cultural thing, but it was just easier for him not to show that perceived weakness with a man, even if I'd had a glimpse of it when all this business had first kicked off.

I grabbed my phone as they came back in, made myself busy looking up directions to the louage station. "Everything okay?"

"All good, man. Thanks," Oz said, his eyes red.

"The louage station is about a kilometre and a half from here. I think we should go down there and see when they're likely to leave in the morning. Then maybe grab some lunch. What do you guys say?"

"Sounds good. Give me two minutes to wash up." said Deniz, wandering into the bathroom and whistling at all the marble.

"Sure. I'll wait outside."

"I'll come with you, Seb," Oz said.

We stood out front, under the welcome shade of a twin-trunked palm, the sputtering water of a white stone fountain, along with the chirping and wingbeats of tiny birds, cutting through the silence.

"Did you see me?" Oz said, looking out toward the road.

"How do you mean?"

"Crying in there. Like a fucking baby."

"Mate. If I was in your shoes, I'd be bawling permanently. You don't need to be ashamed, and you *definitely* don't need to be sorry. Give me a hug, arsehole!"

He embraced me and squeezed. Deniz coming out of the glazed door saved me from internal injuries.

"Which way?" she said, slipping on her sunglasses.

"Follow me." I led them out to the main road.

***

"Where are the louages?" asked Deniz, sipping from her cola bottle during our light lunch in the centre.

I pointed to the other side of the road, where a sandy layby housed three estate cars, painted in brilliant white, with a red stripe down the side. The drivers stood outside, smoking under the shelter of a clump of date palms.

"And which one's going to Kairouan?"

I finished the last mouthful of my sandwich. "There'll be a sign in the window. But I can't read them from here." I strained. Shook my head. "Let's finish our lunch and walk over."

We ate up, thanked the owner of the small sandwich stand, and strolled over the quiet road to the louage drivers.

"Anglais?" I asked.

"Un peu," said the older of the three drivers, stubbing out his cigarette on the tree trunk and dropping the butt into a storm drain.

"Okay. We want to go to Kairouan, tomorrow morning," I said.

One of the younger men stepped forward, wagging his finger back and forth. "No, no. Impossible." He stepped forward. "Is dangereaux!" He pointed to Oz and Deniz in turn. "Yes. Yes"—then to me—"no."

I turned back to the older man, tugged at my shorts. "I'll change my clothes. I can wear a head scarf."

The man leaned back against the tree. "Kairouan road … terrorism. Not like the non-believers. The outsiders. Stop my louage with guns. Monsieur change clothes. But they will know. You are outsider! They will see you as colonist!"

I sighed, exasperated. "I have … *we* have a meeting tomorrow morning. With the imam of the great mosque."

"You go to the *Uqba*?"

I nodded. "Yes. It's *very* important."

"Important for you. Important for me is nobody shoot my car."

Deniz must have seen my temper flaring. She walked over, placed a hand on my shoulder and pushed me gently backwards. "Seb, why don't you let me go there with Oz? I know what questions to ask, I speak Arabic. It might just be easier."

I led her back to the roadside. "Look, Oz is my friend. I feel like I need to be there to support him."

"I get that. I do. But *someone* needs to be physically there, in Kairouan, more than anything. If there's no way for you to get there, this might be the only way." She grabbed my hand. "I know you're doing this for Oz. And I know he'd feel better with you there, rather than just me and him but …" She looked over her shoulder at the drivers. "Don't get angry and burn our bridges, okay? Ibrahim warned us about this."

I forced my features into a smile. She was completely right. We walked back over. "Thank you," I said. "We will try to find an alternative, but if it's not possible, my friends will travel without me. When is the earliest morning trip?"

"Five-thirty. Then another before eight. What time your meeting?"

"Eleven-thirty. Plenty of time. Thank you, again."

We moved away from the layby and onto the main road, heading back toward the apartment.

"Are you okay if I can't make it?" I said to Oz.

"It's better you come. But if they won't take you, okay. I go with Deniz."

"I'm sorry. I really wanted to be there for you."

Oz stopped walking. "You can't be sorry. All this is impossible without you. If you hadn't arranged all this, Sila already has no hope. Thank you." He placed one hand over his heart and the other on my shoulder.

I caught Deniz's eye, and she smiled at me.

"I'll make sure we get what we need," she said.

***

We took the afternoon for some much-needed relaxation, taking turns to play selections from Spotify playlists on the connected hi-fi set up in the apartment, while we sipped some cold but unremarkable local Celtia beers. As the sun sank rapidly beyond the horizon and the lights of the pool area below bathed the complex in an off-white glow, I sat at the dining table with Oz, checking the details of everything that had happened so far. Deniz made notes, ensuring she understood everything clearly and in detail. There was no way of knowing, but we couldn't be sure Imam Kalifi would understand English, much less Turkish, so it would be up to Deniz to communicate in my absence.

With her exhaustive questions answered and notes fully taken, we strolled out to the roadside and hailed a tuk-tuk to carry us the short ride up to the marina.

It was all sweeping curves in gleaming white. Restaurants, bars, and a small amusement park at one side, heaving with people and bubbling with conversation and laughter. We ate at a fairly simple grill restaurant, where I chose some lamb kofta with harissa and yoghurt dressing, while my friends opted for the vegetable couscous with a spicy honey chicken tagine.

"I like this," said Oz, placing his knife and fork back down on his plate and taking a swig of his beer.

"The food?" I asked.

"No. Well … yes, actually. But I mean the place. Nice country. Even this shithole." He made air quotes around the label I'd ascribed to Sousse before we arrived.

"I wish we could see more of it together. Had more time. All three of us." A bell rang out as I spoke. I spun in my seat and saw a man in traditional dress walking into the square where the restaurants' tables were laid out carrying a huge wicker basket.

"Who's that guy?" said Deniz.

"You'll smell it soon enough," I said, smiling.

She turned up her nose and sniffed. "Wow, jasmine. Beautiful!"

"Want some? It's dirt cheap."

The two of them shrugged, so I fished out my wallet and beckoned to the man. I caught his eye and he hurried over, the smell wafting over us in a wave.

"One?" he said, holding out a three-headed stem of the flower. I shook my head.

"Three, please."

"Three! Yes, very good." He reached into the basket and pulled out two more clumps, smelling each theatrically before handing them over. "This one … you put in your wife's hair." He gestured toward Deniz.

"Oh … we're not …" I began.

"Not married? Better." He laughed, then looked at Deniz imploringly. "Is tradition, madame," he said, thrusting the jasmine into my hand and closing my fingers around it.

"Come on then," Deniz said, leaning forward and turning her head slightly. I gently brushed back her hair and fed the stem of the flowers through it, behind her ear, then combed down the tresses with my fingers to keep it in place.

"There," I said, then blushed as our eyes met at such close quarters.

"Thank you," she said. "Smells absolutely divine."

Oz sniffed his own sprig, closing his eyes and savouring the scent.

I reached into my wallet and pulled out a note, handing it to the man.

"Nothing smaller?" he said, a sour expression pulling at his aged features.

"I'm sorry, I spent all my coins earlier in the day. You can keep it."

"*This?*" He wagged his finger. "Too much. Come with me. We take change in restaurant."

"Fair enough," I said, standing and following him to the waiter at the till. He spoke in rapid fire Arabic, pointing to me and our table, then shaking his basket. The waiter gave a tired looking shake of his head, then went further inside, calling out for someone.

As soon as the waiter had gone, the vendor looked both ways, then said, "You need a ride to Kairouan, tomorrow, yes?"

"Ye-wait, what? How did you—"

"Quiet. My cousin is louage driver. He told me. You're not hard to find. The British and two Turks."

"How do I know you're not … never mind."

"With the Salafists? Ha! They don't come to the tourist places with flowers. They bring … something else."

"That's not what I meant."

"Oh?"

"We're going to Kairouan because … my friend … his family is having problems with … a djinn."

The man spat into a nearby plant pot. "Inshallah, the djinn never crossed my path." He nodded toward the returning waiter at the back of the restaurant. "We don't have a lot of time." He scribbled a number on the waiter's discarded notepad and ripped it off. "My mobile number. I go to Kairouan tomorrow to make a delivery. I am from Berber people. I take silver pieces for a shop there. I can take you. Hidden."

The waiter outstretched his hand and dropped a pile of coins into the tip tray. The man took a few then handed the tray to me.

"No, really. Keep it," I said. "Shukran."

I returned to my table. "Looks like I might be able to join you both tomorrow after all."

# Chapter Eight

Oz checked his watch for the seventh time, smoking aggressively. "The louage will be gone by now," he said. "What time this guy say he'd be here?"

I checked my phone. No new messages or calls. "Around eight."

"You gave him the correct location?"

I nodded. "The address *and* a GPS pin. He'll be here."

"I hope so," he said and stubbed out his cigarette, blowing a plume of white smoke into the air, dragon-like.

"Maybe you should call again," said Deniz with a tortured expression, accentuated by her voluminous hair being pinned uncomfortably under a headscarf.

I hit redial and waited as the tone buzzed in my ear. A horn tooted to my right, further up the road. It was a small truck, the flatbed at the rear covered with a framed canopy. The driver waved. It was him. I hung up the phone and moved to the roadside.

"Sorry for the late," he said as he stopped the truck and stepped out. "My brother was helping me loading the silver pieces. I am Anir."

He offered his hand to Deniz then to Oz. "We don't waste any more time," he said and led me to the rear of the truck.

He pointed to a spot near to the cab, sheltered from the sun and from other travellers by the canopy and stacked boxes of goods.

I climbed in and sat on the piled blankets he'd prepared for me. I heard him direct Oz then Deniz into the passenger seats up front and we were on our way.

After a few minutes of noisy scooters and horns blaring, the sounds of the city dulled beneath the persistent growl of the truck's ancient diesel engine. I watched the ivory apartment blocks and municipal buildings shrink into the distance until all that remained was the long sliver of asphalt, cutting through a barren, sandy landscape. Leaning against the wall of the cab, I thought about our meeting with the imam. And about how far we'd come since the widow had turned Oz's world—and subsequently my own—on its head.

After around half an hour, I felt a jolt in the otherwise smooth drive, before we gradually came to a stop. The engine cut out. I held my position. Listened. There were voices outside the truck, talking in Arabic. They were speaking far too quickly for me to grasp what they were saying. Then they stopped. Heavy footsteps rounded the side of the vehicle until I saw a pair of navy trousers topped with a sky-blue shirt come into view. Police.

I took a breath, tried to make myself as small as possible. Then I heard a volley of Arabic, followed by the words I'd been dreading, in French. "Get out of there. Slowly. Hands up!"

I did as I was asked, of course, and found a second officer standing alongside Anir, fiddling with some papers. Deniz and Oz watched on, while the stocky officer nearest to me trained her gun on me, her expression inscrutable through her dark sunglasses.

She demanded my ID. I slowly slipped my hand into the pocket of my trousers, not wanting to give her a reason to open fire, then pulled out my passport and wallet. I handed them over. She spent a moment looking them over, flicking several times between the photo page and the visa stamp from when I'd entered the country.

"Why were you in there?" she asked.

"The louage drivers wouldn't take us. They're worried about people like me on the road to Kairouan. The Salafists—"

"The Salafists are under control," she said, then made a hand signal to her partner that I didn't understand. "Why *are* you going to Kairouan?"

"We have an appointment to see Imam Kalifi at the Uqba."

She took off her sunglasses. "You?"

"Yes. My friend is an expert on scripture and—"

"Okay!" She held up her hand. Clearly, she'd heard enough of my story. She paced back across to Anir and unleashed a barrage of unintelligible Arabic at him, then wrote him a ticket. From the look on Deniz's face, she wasn't being very polite.

Anir thanked them both, bowing his head gently, before the two officers got into their car and drove off.

"I am sorry," Anir said. "They do this because I am Berber. The authorities … do not accept us."

"I can't believe the way she spoke to you," said Deniz. "That's the closest I've come to wanting to hit a police officer."

"Good that you didn't," said Oz. "How much time do we have?"

"Plenty of time," I said. "Close to two hours and we can't be much more than twenty kilometres away, right, Anir?"

He nodded.

"By the way, how much was the ticket?"

Anir shrugged his shoulders. "Not much. Don't worry."

"Uh-uh, forget it. You're doing us a huge favour, I'll get it." I took the paper. "This is fifty euros! That's a big fine here." I reached into my wallet, pulled out two hundred-dinar bills and handed them over. "Please take it."

Anir stuffed the money into his pocket. "Shukran. Now, let's get you to Kairouan." As he spoke, a motorcycle screamed out of what looked like a small livestock farm at the side of the road and flew up the deserted road.

"Someone's in a hurry," I said.

Anir's face was pale. "I hope … no matter. Come on. Let's go, quickly." He ushered the others into the vehicle, then shot me a look that told me I should quicken my pace. I leapt in and clambered my way to the back, the vehicle already rolling off the shoulder before I could sit.

Where the journey so far had been smooth and gentle, now the acceleration was sharper, gear shifts hurried, the truck and its contents juddering each time. Anir's panic was transmitted to me. I reached for my phone and opened the maps app. Still twenty-one kilometres from the Kairouan city limits. Between our location and destination, there was nothing but arid desolation with the odd small holding or warehouse.

Despite my lack of faith, I scrunched my eyes closed and offered up prayers to whatever forces governed the universe. I focussed on the rumble of tyres on tarmac, of the engine's persistent, guttural growl. My breathing slowed, along with my heart rate. Fifteen minutes more, that was all we needed.

A throatier tone began to sing in disharmony with the truck. Another voice joined, the two similar but not the same. They were behind me as I faced the back of the vehicle. One shifted to my left. The truck jolted hard toward the shoulder and back again. The squeal of metal on metal rang out, before the whine of the smaller engine rose to a scream that faded quickly. I lunged forward onto my hands and knees, peered around the boxes which had obscured my view and saw a man dressed all in black clothing still rolling along the road. Sparks glowed like fireworks, even against the brightness of the day, as his bike slid away from him. Still the other bike engine persisted behind me.

I shifted back, trying to return to my seat. Then a single gunshot cracked the air, followed by the sound of breaking glass, and Anir slammed on the brakes. The van screeched forwards and I tumbled, my head smashing into the metal barrier between the two sections of the truck.

I picked myself up, not sure if I'd blacked out. A voice was shouting at the front. All Arabic, my head far too confused to even attempt deciphering it. I heard the doors open and slam. Then more shouting. I crawled to the rear of the truck and slowly lowered my legs toward the ground.

I pushed off and landed soundlessly. The shouting continued. No response from my friends or Anir were forthcoming. I pressed myself to the rear wall of the truck and slid alongside it, peering around the edge.

The man was younger than I'd guessed. His beard was long but patchy and his black clothes hung from his lean body. His fingers twitched on the rifle he was holding. I felt relieved not to see an automatic, which I'd feared after reading about the attacks a few years earlier.

He was speaking more calmly now, though his tone remained harsh. I heard him mention Kairouan and he referred to his 'brother' more than once, likely referring to the man on the other bike, who Anir had run off the road. He made to turn toward me, and I darted back behind the line of the truck. His footfalls scuffed at the sandy shoulder of the road, and I flinched back as quickly and silently as I could manage.

I crept around to the right side of the vehicle and crouched. Watched as his feet turned to the rear of the van. He yelled into the back of the van, poked at the boxes with the barrel of his gun, the silver goods clanging around.

Seizing my chance, I took a step toward him and kicked as hard as I could with the flat of my foot into the side of the knee joint. His leg crumpled beneath him, and the gun went off again. Anir sprinted around from the other side of the vehicle and wrestled the weapon from the fallen man. He brought the butt of the rifle down onto his temple as he tried to scramble to his feet. The man collapsed, out cold.

Anir pulled back the latch and worked another bullet into the chamber, then held it close to the front tyre of the bike and blasted a hole in it. As he lowered the rifle, I noticed a trickle of blood meandering down Anir's forearm.

"Anir, you're bleeding," I said.

"He missed me. Glass from the mirror."

I glanced over at the wing mirror; only fragments of glass remained around the edge of the frame.

He passed me the weapon. "Take this. We must go. *Now!* There could be more."

I didn't need telling twice. I climbed aboard and hurried to my spot. The truck engine started, and we pulled away in a cloud of sandy dust. The motionless assailant and his damaged bike lay still as they disappeared from sight.

My hands were still trembling as we entered one of the gates in the old city walls. Even in their partially collapsed state, the towering blocks of sandstone which loomed over the entry road told us we had arrived in an ancient place. I edged toward the rear opening of the truck, to give myself a better view.

The breeze of the open road died the moment we crossed the threshold, the temperature rising from regular desert heat to something even more oppressive. The road angled downward, toward the centre of the town, along the street where the butchers' shops were located. The metallic tang of the blood draining from the hanging carcasses of cows and goats filled my nostrils and, combined with the oppressive heat and the stillness in the air, I found myself having to fight the will to vomit.

We slowed as the road undulated upwards again, moving away from the built-up trade centre. The huge cobbles of the antique surface rattled my bones through the indelicate chassis of the truck. Mercifully, the fragrance of blood had dispersed, or I really would have thrown up.

We moved back onto tarmac, and I caught sight of the first sections of the inner-city walls, protecting the *uqba* itself. We passed a handful of pilgrimage buses before crawling to a halt in the square in front. I climbed out and rounded the vehicle.

"Thank you, Anir, so much," I said from the passenger window and appraised the damage caused by the fracas in closer detail. "What do we owe you? For diesel?"

He waved his hand in my direction. "Not much. Don't worry. We talk about this later. You have my number. Call me when your meeting is over. I will deliver my things, take lunch, then wait."

"Will you be able to treat the cut on your wrist?"

He waved his head around in a non-committal response.

I opened the door, and Oz and Deniz stepped out. The three of us gazed up at the sandstone structure towering over us.

"Wow," said Deniz. "This building has been here for over a thousand years. Imagine."

"Some of the gravestones are just as old, too. I saw them last time." I pointed to the featureless, uniform blocks of white stone in front of the mosque. I turned to Oz, squeezed his shoulder. "Are you ready for this? After coming all this way?"

"I'm ready."

"Then let's go."

# CHAPTER FIVE

"So, where do we meet our guy?" Deniz said, her gaze still fixed upon the towering, cuboid minaret.

"Well, not inside. I can't even enter prayer halls in this country."

"Courtyard then? It's still only ten to eleven."

I had no better ideas, so we paid the tourist entry fee and stepped under the ancient, arched gate. As we moved into the courtyard, the sounds of the road were hushed. The chugging of the buses and murmur of conversation died away until all that was left were the whispering wind and the wingbeats of flocks of birds which soared overhead at irregular intervals.

None of us said a word.

I couldn't speak for the others, but as I stood there in that silent, contemplative space, my mind reached back over those last ten days and the events which had led us there. Events which I would have called impossible on that night when the widow wove her spell, or whatever it was. I thought about how incredibly strong—normal even—Oz had been. I'm not sure I would have held it together, had it been my niece in the hospital bed. I thought, too, about how chance had thrown Deniz into my path and how much I enjoyed her company, despite the horrors swirling around us.

Footsteps fractured my reverie, clacking on the ancient slabs toward us from the main prayer hall. Wearing an ornate hat, with an attached scarf wrapped around his neck and tucked into his robe, the imam's face was deeply grooved by age, but there was warmth when he smiled.

"Sebastian?" he said, with a French twang. I stepped forward and shook his hand. He placed his hand over mine, greeting me firmly, before turning first to Deniz, then to Oz. The colour seemed to sap from his cheeks, eyes glazing over. "I am so very sorry," he managed in heavily accented English.

The look that passed between them was intense. I found my eyes meeting Deniz's, seemingly unsure of how to react. I cleared my throat, switched to French and asked where we should conduct the meeting. Kalifi rubbed his long beard, then led us through a side gate and into a single-story building which formed part of the defensive wall. The small noticeboard inside told us it was a local community centre of sorts. He spoke to the man at the desk, who gazed at the imam reverentially, then led us through the back to a counselling room, gesturing for us to sit around an oval table.

"Tell me everything," he said. I explained that Oz was unable to speak French and had very little Arabic, but between Deniz and myself, we spent the next thirty minutes recounting the disturbing episodes which had led us there. When we were finished, silence descended over the room while he considered what we'd said.

Finally, he asked me what we wanted.

My mouth opened, but I couldn't find the words. Eventually, I told him I wasn't a believer—at least never had been before all of this—but that I supposed what we were looking for was a weapon. An exorcism. A way to break whatever spell was binding that eleven-year-old girl in the hospital in Dalaman to her coma. I felt my throat strain as emotion—despair or anger, I still don't know to this day—crept into my tone. I cut myself off, apologised, then simply stopped talking.

When he spoke again, it was in Arabic to Deniz. He continued for several minutes, uninterrupted. When he stopped, his face was flushed, tears covering his eyes in a glossy sheen under the flicker of the strip lighting.

"I don't know if you're ready for this," Deniz said. "I *wasn't* ready for this."

Oz, somehow the calmest of us, outwardly at least, sat forward on his chair. "Ready." He forced a smile.

"He says the djinn have been on the earth for longer than the faith. Longer than people. That there have been those who have wielded power over some of them, but little of that is understood. When you asked for an exorcism, Seb, he said it almost made him laugh. So many movies, from all backgrounds, make it seem like the dark powers can be *cast out* by a priest, a rabbi or an imam with a book of spells."

She paused then, eyes flicking back across to the old man's. He gave a gentle nod and waved his hand, urging her on.

"The words of the scripture can be a weapon. The dark ones—and let's remember that if this is one of the ghul, it's among the most corrupt entities from the deepest pit of the dark ones—don't like them. But it's not a cure-all. It's not like he comes to Turkey, says the words, and takes a nice holiday while Sıla goes back to school. At best, the exorcism removes the djinn from the body. But it's impossible to say whether it will go right back in after we're done. Only then it's angrier than ever. And, finally, much of what's happened suggests that the djinn might well be feeding off her, but not possessing her body. It's taken too much direct action against us. It's in the world. It's active. The imam's advice is to steer clear of it. Stop engaging. Hope it releases Sıla when it gets bored."

I held my head in my hands. That *wasn't* a solution. "So, how do we kill it?" I said through the spaces between my fingers.

Deniz shuddered. "I don't think it's a good i—"

"How do we kill it?" I asked Kalifi in French, and immediately felt Oz's hand squeezing my arm. The old cleric clicked his tongue, then reached into a pocket in his robe, pulling out a coiled piece of very old looking parchment.

"I knew this would be the question weeks ago, when we first spoke," he said. "I thought there was no answer. Kill a being as old as the land beneath our feet? A being with all the corrupt power of the fallen at its fingertips? A being that knows of death only through dealing it out to we mortals, whether for vengeance or by whim? I was sure it couldn't be done. Sure it *hadn't* been done."

"It has though, hasn't it?" I was on my feet now, leaning over the artefact, its script faded to a faint purple as the indigo had faded with time.

"One man. A warrior, then later, what you would term a monk, saw such darkness unfolding. He was on a pilgrimage here from Mamluk Egypt. His party were struck time and again, by disease, freak sandstorms, insects and, finally, one of those close to him was rendered comatose. His party stopped at an oasis, and he meditated, trying to divine how to rid himself of this scourge. Then he had his realisation."

"Which was?"

"He invited the djinn in. Offered himself to it. His body, mind, spirit. Every part of him."

"How does that—?"

"Before the creature could fully take hold, imbuing him with its dark power and rendering him almost immortal, his wife sliced off his head with his own scimitar, then burned the body to the bones on a pyre, there in the desert. It's written that the foul screams as it died could be heard from as far away as Alexandria."

I slumped back in my seat.

"What must we do?" said Oz.
I had no answers.

# Chapter Ten

Kalifi offered to show us a tea house near the Uqba, but when he suggested Deniz might not be able to enter a predominantly male space in such a conservative city, we politely declined. We shuffled outside while he had the receptionist make us a copy of the scroll he'd shown us at the meeting. He handed it over, assured me he would still be on hand to field any questions which might crop up, then wished us well. We moved away from the grand mosque area toward the modern part of the town.

My phone buzzed in my pocket while we walked. "It's Ibrahim," I said and walked a few steps ahead. "Give me some good news, my friend." There was a long pause at the other end of the line.

"I have news. I don't exactly know if it's good or bad. Midou received the samples of the curse fabric from the lab this morning."

"Go on."

"It's old. Between twelfth and fourteenth centuries. Silk, gold thread, and the seed and soil particles on it are almost certainly from upper Egypt. Cairo, Alexandria ..."

"Fucking hell."

"Ah, so it's bad news?"

I made a sound somewhere between laughing and choking. "Truth is, Ibrahim, I don't really know. Look, we're just out of our meeting. I'm going to get back to the others. But thank you, really."

"Yes, of course. Anything I can do. Look after yourselves. Talk soon." He hung up.

I slowed my walking pace and returned to the others just as we entered the grid of narrow streets in the newer part of the city. We followed our noses and found a simple family restaurant nestled in a side road.

I was conscious of the myriad eyes scanning my features as we ordered. I pointed out a table tucked away in the far corner, and Deniz was kind enough to go and order us some lunch while I sat with Oz and explained the finer details of the meeting. If his confidence was dented during the audience with the imam, by the time I was finished his complexion had returned to the pallor I'd seen a week earlier, when we'd been reunited in Istanbul.

He leant forward, mouth open as if to speak, but saying nothing. Not wanting to pressure him, I remained silent.

"Lentil soup is the best thing they have, according to that guy." Deniz nodded her head toward a heavyset, elderly man sat on the sole bar stool at the counter.

He touched his finger to his cap and smiled as we caught his eye. He wasn't wrong, either.

"You've told him then?" Deniz said as she tore into a flat bread and soaked one end in the vibrantly orange liquid.

"He told me, yes. But I don't understand. He told me the situation—his opinion of the situation—but what about advice? We come for practical advice, no?"

"He did give us advice, in a manner of speaking. To leave it well alone. Not piss it off," I said.

"Eloquently put, Seb." Deniz eyed me harshly, shaking her head. "But he's right. Kalifi's advice was, basically, that if we mess with this thing, based on how vicious it's been so far ..." She trailed off.

"And Sıla? She just ... stays ... like that?"

I lowered my eyes to my bowl, knowing that were it a member of my family paralysed by some curse or other, I wouldn't accept being told to leave it alone. Beyond that, I'd promised to help Oz. I'd been so sure this path would lead us to the answers we needed, but instead we were staring at another brick wall. I'd failed him.

"She can't stay like that. We have to find a way. This is a setback, nothing more." I felt Deniz's eyes on me as she spoke, willing me to agree or make a suggestion as I ate a few more spoonfuls of my soup.

"Was that Ibrahim's guy—what was his name? Midou? —on the phone? Did he say anything about where the curse fabric in the museum had come from?" Deniz said.

"It was Ibrahim, yeah. Midou's test results estimated the fabric's age at between nine hundred and eleven hundred years and said the particles they found on the material were consistent with upper Egypt at that … Oh."

"Yes, exactly. *Oh*."

"Oh … what?" Oz shovelled down half of the soup, then asked us again.

"Kalifi's story about the Mamluk. But I don't know if we should just be hightailing it off to Egypt."

"We've got nothing else to go on. What do you think we should do?"

I took a moment to consider the question.

"Stay here for now. Go back to Tunis, talk to Ibrahim and his guy. Do some research about this Mamluk saint before we go to another new country. Egypt isn't as safe as it once was. Not travelling independently."

The others were silent, Oz finishing up his soup.

"I'm not saying we don't go. I'm saying we prepare first. Let's head back to Sousse with Anir and we can discuss it better there."

***

Anir waved away my attempts to pay for his new wing mirror, claiming he was on good terms with a mechanic and he'd done it for the price of a brique lunch. When I saw I wasn't going to be able to persuade him otherwise, I rounded the small pick-up and went to climb aboard. The boxes I'd hidden behind on the way into the city were all gone.

"Anir, where am I supposed to hide?"

He shrugged his shoulders. "We leave Kairouan now. Salafists will be happy."

I couldn't really argue with that. I hopped in and moved to the corner before pulling a scratchy blanket up over my legs in a half-hearted attempt to remain inconspicuous. The engine started up, doors slammed, and we were on our way.

The road was quiet, as our Berber guide had suggested, with no violent incidents like the one we'd experienced on the way to the holy city. I was able to pass the time looking out at the sandy horizon, dotted with patches of greenery as we crossed rivers, and consider what our next steps might be. Whether, as Kalifi had advised, it might not be better to leave the djinn well alone and hope that it would tire of us and free Sıla from her comatose state.

Deniz had the bit between her teeth, though. She was determined to act, so much so I feared she would go in blind, despite not knowing what we might face, or *how* we might confront it.

Oz, I could understand. It was his flesh and blood in jeopardy. For now, at least, the only child in the next generation of his family. His rushes of blood were only natural. I had to convince Deniz to slow down, do this the right way, before we were all flung into harm's way.

***

The pick-up rolled to a gentle stop at the bus stop just down from the louage station. I hopped out and moved around the side of the vehicle to stand with my companions.

"Sure I can't give you something toward the mirror?" I said hopefully.

Anir waved his hand dismissively. "I hope the imam at the Uqba had the answers you needed." He reached out and clutched Oz's hand. "Inshallah, everything turns out for the best, my friend."

Oz's face flushed.

We thanked Anir and watched the pick-up disappear down the road, before crossing over and making the short walk to the apartment. When we arrived, I fired up my laptop and handed beers around to the others. We crowded around the table on the balcony, the balmy heat still quite oppressive, even in the shade as the sun had begun its descent on the other side of the building.

I opened a browser window and clicked in the search bar. The cursor flickered.

"I don't even know what I'm really looking for," I said. "I've got no experience in Egypt. No contacts, nothing." I ran my fingers through my hair, the stress of the situation finally catching up with me. Deniz stood, took a sip from her beer, then bashed into my shoulder with her hip.

"Okay, up. Time out for you, mister. My turn. I know a few people. And I wrote an essay *way* back where I needed some advice on Mamluk poetry from a lady at the American University in Cairo."

I opened my mouth to respond.

"Shut up, Seb. Sit over there, drink your beer. Let your brain unravel a bit. I'll do some of the heavy lifting for once. Tell him, Oz."

Oz looked surprised to be called upon, but quickly fixed a smile to his face and guided me to the seat on the other side of the table. Once I'd sat, he moved over to his rucksack and began rummaging around.

"Ah, here," he said, and held up his backgammon board. "Let's play outside, leave Deniz to work."

I grabbed our beer bottles and slid open the balcony door. "Good luck," I told Deniz, with a wink. We sat down to play, and I was soon engrossed in the game, quickly realising this kind of distraction was exactly what I'd needed. How Oz managed to distract himself with all that was going on back home, I couldn't say. But I didn't ask. Didn't feel the need to. We threw the dice around, competed fiercely, and taunted one another with every victory. An hour turned into two, until the door slid open.

"Are you guys staying out here all night?" Deniz said, loosening her hair from its braid. "I've sent emails to three different people at the university, two I know and one I don't, but she's new and big on Arabic scripture. I've also got some places that might be worth checking out in the citadel in Cairo."

"You *have* been busy. Sounds like a productive session."

She cricked her neck and grimaced. "Yeah, but now I need a shower and some food. What's the dinner plan?"

I shrugged. "No plan. Marina again?"

Deniz made a face. "It's so *fake*. What about the old city? There must be some good spots."

"I'll get on Tripadvisor while you shower, see what I can find."

"Deal."

✳✳✳

We returned from dinner, well fed courtesy of a tiny couscous restaurant, which was in fact more like a cupboard. Only two dishes on the menu, hand scribbled on the back of a flier for the city market, but made with the freshest stuff that the owner, Aziz, could get his hands on. Delicious, plentiful, and embarrassingly cheap.

Deniz and I spent most of the hour discussing a strategy for further information gathering before we headed over to

94

Cairo, while Oz had been in incredibly cheerful form, making jokes and recounting his often-catastrophic attempts to get Marie's attention back in his army days in Zonguldak.

"I think I'm going to turn in," I said, dozing off at one end of the plush white sofa.

"I won't be far behind," said Deniz. "I should have washed my hair, but it can wait for the morning."

We both naturally turned to Oz. He stood gazing out of the balcony doors, his complexion warmed by the yellow light cast from the pool illumination.

"I think I'm going to sit up longer, guys. I was thinking of writing an email to Marie. Can I use one of your laptops?"

Deniz was quicker than me and my sleep-addled head, dashing over to the small dining table and signing in. She turned the computer to him, then squeezed his shoulder. "Help yourself. But do get some rest. We don't know how long before we'll be back on the move."

"I will. Just an hour. No more."

"Good night, buddy," I said. "See you in the morning."

# Chapter Eleven

"Seb! Seb, wake up!"

I jolted in bed, my vision fogged, no light creeping in between the blinds. Deniz stood over me, her curls bound in a wrap. I swiftly pulled up the thin sheet to cover my modesty.

"Morning. Everything okay?" I rubbed my bleary eyes, switched on the light.

Then I noticed the tears streaking her face.

"Hey, hey. What's up?" I stood, placed one hand on her cheek.

She tried to respond, choked, then gulped a breath of air and tried again. "It's … it's Oz. He's gone."

"Gone? What do you mean 'gone'? Like, gone for a swim or a walk?" I stepped into my shorts and clumsily pulled the previous day's T-shirt over my head.

"Look." She thrust a page, torn from her notebook, into my chest and bit her lip.

My heart thumped as my eyes frantically scanned the scrawl on the page. Then I reached the midway point and a hammer blow struck me in my gut, the air leaving my lungs involuntarily. My hands shook and I, too, felt tears welling in my eyes.

"No. No, no, no, no, no!" I stalked to the lounge and slammed the page down onto the dining table. I tugged desperately at my hair, then moved to the kitchen, clutching my phone and thumbing at the screen with trembling fingers which refused to obey my commands. I found Oz in the contacts and hit call.

Switched off.

"Fuck!" I screamed and dropped to my knees.

I felt Deniz's hand on my back and the rage seeped away, a wave of desperation flooding in to fill the gap it had left.

"Just why? Fucking why?" I said in a hoarse, fractured voice.

"You know why. We both do."

I stood. "But we could have … we could *still* …"

"I know. I know." She pulled me closer, her hand at my face, pulling it into her shoulder, the fragrance of jasmine still alive in her hair. I sobbed, the force of it shaking my entire form. She squeezed me tighter until I had nothing left to give up.

Finally, I stepped back, wiping my sore eyes. "What do we do now?"

"There are only a few airlines serving Egypt from here. We find them. Figure out the way he might have gone and work from there. I'll fire up the laptop. You get some coffee on. We're going to need it."

I looked at my watch. 5:07a.m. I prepared the stove-top coffee maker with a generous pile of strong coffee grounds and put it on the hob, before picking up the note Oz had left and reading over it once more.

*Seb and Deniz,*

*You've done everything you can, bringing me all this way and helping me. But you can't do more now. You listened to the advice of the Imam. The only way to be sure is to follow the example of the Mamluk from the past. I'm going to Egypt. I will find the djinn, invite it into me and do what I must. I wrote an email to Marie to explain to her. I hope she will forgive me after some time.*

*Don't try to follow me. You won't convince me to change my plan. It's the only way.*
*Thank you again.*
*Your friend,*
*Özgur*

# Part Two

Shadow of the Hidden

# Chapter Twelve

I frantically scoured the apartment for clues while Deniz prepared coffee. I soon discovered Oz had taken his return ticket to Istanbul, though that wasn't much help in tracking him to Cairo. Deniz powered up her laptop and began looking at her recently accessed files. Sure enough, he'd been through some of the saved maps and notes with addresses and contacts. She scribbled down a few notes in a pad, then checked which airports had flights to Cairo that day.

Frustratingly, there were three of them. We ruled out Djerba immediately, assuming he wouldn't want to go to all the trouble of taking the ferry to the island to the south. That left us with Hammamet, only sixty kilometres away, or the main hub of Tunis, where we'd flown in days earlier. On consulting the schedule, we found that the only flight of the day had left Hammamet thirty minutes earlier. Tunis had an early evening flight. I handed Deniz my card and passport to book us some seats and began to throw my things into a bag.

Within thirty minutes, we were out on the dusty road at the front of the apartment complex, hailing a cab as the first cracks of the morning sun rose over the whitewashed walls. The third car we waved to was empty and stopped. Deniz jumped in first and shuffled along while I loaded the rucksacks into the boot.

"La Gare, s'il vous plaît," I said as I sat beside her. The driver was rolling off again before I'd even closed the door behind me. I grabbed my phone and found Ibrahim in my phonebook. He answered after a single ring.

"Seb, my boy, tell all," he said in a typically jovial tone.

I could almost see his face fall as I explained what had transpired over the past twenty-four hours.

"Do you need any help? Somewhere to stay? Flights arranged?"

"We've handled all that. I just wanted to let you know. And to ask you to keep us informed if you get any more leads about that curse fragment."

"Of course. Dear lord, I do hope you find him. His poor family have been through enough."

"I know, man. He thinks it's the only thing he can do. Thinks he *has* to do this."

Ibrahim remained quiet on the other end of the phone.

"We're almost at the station. I'll stay in touch, okay?"

"Take care, Seb, and if you need anything at all …"

"You've done more than enough already. But thank you."

I hung up the phone as we swung into the taxi bay at the front of the main station. I handed the driver a couple of notes and followed Deniz into the forecourt.

"I'll get tickets," she said. "Stay here." She dropped her rucksack at my feet and scurried off to join the short queue.

I scanned the departures board above me, finding two trains north to the capital in the next couple of hours, even if we missed the one that left in fifteen minutes. A wave of relief washed over me, but was soon replaced with a pain in my gut as my mind switched from worrying about making a flight to my friend's attempted suicide—or worse.

"Got 'em. Let's go," Deniz waved the white airline-style boarding cards at me.

"We've still got a few minutes. More coffee?"

"Good idea, I'm beat."

We stopped off at a kiosk, where I grabbed us each a café au lait and a flatbread with spicy merguez sausages and mustard. We bundled onto the train, dumping our rucksacks in the luggage rack at the end of the carriage, before sitting in the slightly more cramped second-class carriage this time.

The atmosphere buzzed with conversation, interspersed with the tinny sound of people watching videos on their phones. We ate, zombie-like after so little sleep, and were already done with the little picnic by the time the train edged away from the platform. The hum of the engine and the rhythmic thrumming of the rails beneath us soon drowned out the noise of the morning travellers. Deniz, opposite me, pulled out her laptop and began flicking through the various files she'd saved and emails she'd received the day before. My eyes were burning from the lack of sleep, so I elected to leave my electronics stowed in my shoulder bag beside me.

We'd been in motion for fifteen minutes or so when the door at the end of the carriage slid violently open and a heavyset man entered, his bulk scarcely contained in a vest at least a size too small. His eyes fixed on mine, and he lumbered forward, his lip turning up into a snarl. I squirmed in my seat and tapped Deniz's foot with my own. She glanced up from the screen. I nodded toward the approaching goliath, trying to be discreet. She went to turn her head and I reached out my hand, placing it on her forearm.

"Don't draw attention to yourself. He might be …" I trailed off.

She slid a few inches down the seatback and edged along until she could peek around the corner. The moment she did, she jolted back to her position, eyes wide.

"Fuck," she said through gritted teeth.

I was about to respond when the man bellowed, in French, "You!" His forefinger was aimed at my face, his muscular forearm trembling.

I made to stand but he closed the distance between us so quickly, there was nowhere for me to go.

"You're in my seat!"

His breath was violently alcoholic, which combined horribly with his body odour. It was all I could do not to choke as he leaned in toward me. Deniz scrabbled in her bag and found my ticket. My seat was the one next to hers.

I apologised and slipped from beneath the towering giant, planting myself beside Deniz on the seat where her bag had been moments earlier.

"Thank you," the man said, slumping into his seat and immediately dozing off.

I was still trembling. "I thought …"

"I don't blame you," Deniz said, squeezing my hand with hers. "He's going to be okay. We'll find him."

"You really think so."

"I have to keep believing."

The train rolled along for a few moments more.

"Look, Seb, why don't you try to get some sleep?"

I rubbed my face and thought about protesting. But I was shattered. And there was nothing I could do on this train. "You'll wake me if anything happens?"

"Promise."

***

The train juddered to a halt, waking me. "Is everything okay?" I asked, hearing the panic in my own voice.

"Everything's fine. Only one more stop."

I noticed the burly man in my former seat had gone while I slept. "Why do you think it hasn't tried to stop us?"

"I was wondering about that while you were sleeping. Then I remembered all the stories from when I was a kid, and from my studies. The djinn are supremely confident. Utterly convinced of their superiority over humans. If it knows we're going after Oz—and that's still a big if—it will assume it can thwart our plans easily enough."

"Cocky bastard."

Deniz's face darkened. "Do not insult it. We do *not* want to piss it off, remember?"

"I think Oz has already done a good job of that. Somehow."

"And look what happened to him."

The train jerked into motion and the bilingual announcement about the final stop in fifteen minutes blared over the public address. When the muffled voice finished speaking, I tried Oz's phone again. Still dead. I stashed my phone and headed down to the luggage racks to take down our bags.

The late morning air was still fresh and cool in the shady, built-up district around the central station. We decided to grab more coffee and a pastry in a small bakery on the other side of the ornate garden out front. Deniz connected to the Wi-Fi on her laptop and checked her messages, one confirming that her request for a meeting with an expert on Mamluk saints—including the beheaded man Kalifi had mentioned in Kairouan—had been granted.

Her other contact, who she'd met at a conference in the US years earlier, had also sent some initial thoughts on the curse fabric which had shown up at the Bardo.

"Look at this," she said, shuffling onto the small sofa beside me and pulling her laptop screen around so I could see. "The shade of blue which forms the backdrop of the curse material was dominant in Mamluk Egypt between the late thirteenth and mid-fourteenth centuries."

"Fits pretty well with our guy's story."

"Doesn't it? There's more, though. He sent me a link to this prose poem, written by a djinn master in Morocco—"

"A djinn-what? Is this like *Pokemon* or something?"

"Shut up. Just read the poem. The second stanza."

She pulled the screen forward.

"It's in Arabic, Deniz."

She grunted, shaking her head. "Sorry. Okay, listen. 'And when the Saint's head was cleaved from his shoulders, the brother of the wicked djinn who had been slain spat a curse into the desert winds as had never been heard before. The clever widow knew not to repeat those tainted words, instead memorising them and inscribing them on a slip of embroidered silk, which was buried beneath the charred body of her brave husband in the family mausoleum on their return to Cairo.'"

"That is *not* a very catchy poem."

Deniz scowled at me. "I'm translating directly, you know how this stuff goes. But look. This is the thing. This fragment could be it. *Must* be it. The original. Sewn by his wife. The one who killed the djinn."

"How does this help us? *Does* this help us?"

"How do you take control of a djinn? Do you know?"

"Everything I know about this subject, I've learned from you. So, no. Enlighten me."

"The first thing you need is its name."

"And does the curse fabric give us that? Or the poem?"

"No."

"Fuck." I laughed, because it seemed like a better option than crying.

"But this expert in Cairo thinks we can find it from here. We're zeroing in on it."

"We'd better get there fast. Before Oz—"

"Don't even say it."

# Chapter Thirteen

We touched down in Cairo as the curtain of night crept across the sky. We moved swiftly through customs and on to the taxi rank with our rucksacks. The call to prayer, delivered by myriad muffled voices, drifted on the air from the city centre. Gleaming, modern skyscrapers and shimmering, brightly lit minarets painted an eclectic landscape.

A battered Peugeot 409 rolled up, the grinning driver leaning out of the glassless side window. "Yes, please?"

"Central Cairo, please," I said. "We're staying at …" I turned to Deniz. "Where are we staying?"

She shoved me out of the way. "Safir hotel. El Duqqi." She opened the rear door and slid over. I dumped the bags in the boot and sat beside her, then we were off.

The hotel was luxurious. I quizzed Deniz on the cost, but she assured me our room was less than fifty euros a night and we were close enough to see the university of letters, where we would go the following day, from our eighth storey window. I couldn't really argue with that.

After a shower and a fresh set of clothes, Deniz insisted we left the hotel for a stroll on the banks of the Nile— probably just to stop my nervous pacing.

Even at night the dry heat was oppressive, like stepping into an oven. As we walked, Deniz pointed out the main features of the medieval citadel across the water, where the beheaded saint's burnt corpse had supposedly been entombed with the curse fabric.

"The necropolis is huge," she said. "Spread over two or three different sections. I hope we can get a precise location from one of my contacts before we have to go over there. Or at least a general idea."

"I hope so, too. I prefer not to spend too much of my time wandering around the city of the dead. Especially after what we've been through lately."

"Here it's even more complicated than that. The Cairo necropolis is home to about three thousand people."

"Bodies? I thought it'd be more."

"Uh-uh. Not the dead. The living."

"They live there with—"

"Yep. They've nowhere else to go. It's sheltered. Safe— for them at least. We need to get in and out, fast. Before we get noticed."

"Let's hope your guy has what we need."

She led me down to the university building, showing me the department we'd visit the next day, before we looped back around and stopped at a bustling Lebanese restaurant and gorged ourselves on shawarma, hummus and pickled vegetables. By the time we'd finished, the midnight call to prayer was everywhere, each voice competing with the next for the busy streets' attention. We crossed the road to avoid the column of human traffic heading upriver toward one of the larger mosques and quickly arrived at the front of the hotel.

I tried Oz's phone again, something which had become almost as ritualised as the local people and their prayers. Once again, straight to answerphone.

"We're coming to help you, mate. Don't do it. Please don't do it," I said and hung up.

"Excuse me, sir." A man was approaching fast from a position beside the river railing. I looked around, but he was definitely talking to me.

"I'm sorry, I don't have time to—"

"Please, sir." He pointed to his open mouth, his eyes pleading, while his other hand gripped my shoulder firmly.

"I'm afraid I don't have any—"

"Lah shukran," Deniz spoke over me, her tone forceful. She linked her arm with mine and tugged me away, the man's grasp slipping. "Leave my husband alone."

I glanced sideways at her, her expression telling me we were possibly in danger.

"Wait," the man said, stepping into my personal space once more and reaffixing his hand to my shoulder. Annoyed, I shoved him backwards. He stumbled, tripping backwards and landing on his arse. The people milling around us paused and a group of tourist police stationed further upriver, near a group of western fast-food restaurants, started coming our way.

Panicked, I leant forward and offered him a hand to pull him up. He sat, staring at his grazed palms, then a teenage boy who'd been standing at the railings burst past me, almost knocking me off balance. He wrenched Deniz's bag from her shoulder and sprinted through the melee of people. I hauled up the fallen man, who begin to shout through the crowd in Arabic.

"I knew it was a scam. Come on!" Deniz grabbed my arm and dragged me away. We ducked and weaved between the throng of people, all of whom seemed to be moving toward us, slowing us down. I glanced over my shoulder to see the tan-uniformed tourist police looking in my direction, firmly gripping their guns. I hoped they'd get bored or find another distraction.

Finally breaking free of the human traffic, we moved onto the university bridge over the Nile, the river's distinctive scent of balm, silt and waste even more noxious as we crossed it. Deniz wove between stationary traffic ahead of me, car horns blasting. I followed her, the boy with the bag just in sight as he darted into the courtyard of the Salah Al-Din Mosque and disappeared into the building. I stopped to catch my breath and gazed up at the ancient sandstone building, its warm lamps illuminating the minarets like pillars of flame.

"Can we go in?" I said.

"Not dressed like that," Deniz said, pulling at the sleeve of my T-shirt. "They might have something you can borrow, come on."

She lurched toward the entrance. I gulped a lungful of breath and hurried after her.

As we arrived at the entrance, a thickset man stood with his palm raised. He spoke Arabic in harsh, quick tones. Deniz spun on her heels.

"They have shawls, but *you* can't enter during prayers. I can go inside, but I have to go to the women's upper gallery." She ran her fingers through her curls, eyes raised as she thought. She quickly spat a question at the doorman, who answered affirmatively, then she turned back to me. "He says this is the only entrance and exit. I'm going to go in, see if I can spot him from the women's prayer hall. You stay here, if he comes out, don't wait for me. Just get that bag."

"Okay," I said. "Good luck."

I stood outside for about five minutes. The doorman mellowed and offered me a cigarette, which I politely refused. The murmuring sound of the group prayer drifted through the numerous doors between where I stood and the halls within, calming my nerves.

Just as my heart rate was returning to normal, the boy shoved the doorman aside with a grunt and burst away to my left, into the courtyard of the mosque.

I took off after him, the boy zig zagging in and out of the shadows cast by the towering edifice, one moment brightly lit, the next hidden but for the heavy slap of his well-worn trainers on stone. I forced myself into a sprint, reaching out for the wall to pull me round the corner. The boy was heading for the next bridge, taking him off the island and across to the east bank of the Nile. He glanced over his shoulder at me and ran straight into Deniz. They tumbled to the ground, limbs entangled.

She wrenched the bag from his hands, but he tugged at her hair, loosed from its ponytail, then punched her in the stomach. She winced and heat rose up my neck. The boy snatched the bag away once more just as I shoulder barged him to the ground. His head smashed into the pavement, and he stopped moving.

Panic was written into the lines on Deniz's face as she looked first at me, then at the motionless boy. I handed her the bag, then turned him onto his back and checked his airway. He was breathing.

"He's okay," I said, noting the blood seeping from the gash on his left temple. "He'll be fine. Are you alright?" I said and squeezed Deniz's hand in my own. She looked herself up and down, as if only then considering it.

"Just bruises, I think." She squeezed my hand back.

The boy's eyes opened, and he began to speak in Arabic.

"Laqad ta'akhar. Laqad ta'akhar. Laqad ta'akhar. Laqad ta'akhar." His mouth twisted into a sinister leer as he spoke, his pupils heavily dilated.

"What's he saying?" I asked Deniz.

"It's *too late*," she said. "Over and over, the same thing."

"You think he's talking ab—"

"Özgur?" he said. Then he began laughing hysterically, his body writhing on the ground.

I balled my fists, anger boiling inside me, the will to lash out rising. Deniz placed her hands on my shoulders. Pressed her forehead to mine.

"You know it's not him. It's not the boy. It's ... the other thing."

I breathed out a long breath that I'd been holding for I don't know how long and pulled her into an embrace.

"Do you think it is?"

She leaned her head on my chest. "Is what?"

"Too late. For Oz."

"We're here. We'll find him." She glanced down at the boy. He'd gone quiet, the twisted taunt seemingly over. "I think he's going to be fine. Let's get back to the hotel."

# Chapter Fourteen

Our walk back to the hotel was mercifully uninterrupted by beggars or bag snatchers. The streets were infinitely calmer, with evening prayers continuing in the mosques. We were able to take a detour around the botanical gardens, across the road from the zoo, before looping round to the hotel.

"Nightcap?" I asked, eyeing the almost-empty bar near reception.

Deniz groaned. "I could do with a drink, really. But I also want to get into my bed and get cosy, too. What do you say to raiding the minibar?"

"Done. Lead the way." I gestured toward the elevators, and she strode ahead of me, one hand still holding her bag tightly to her body after the robbery. I followed her in and pressed the button for the eighth floor. As we entered, Deniz headed for the bathroom to check on her bruises.

"What do you want to drink?" I yelled through the closed door.

"Gin, whisky, whatever they've got."

I knelt at the desk and opened the minifridge. "Oh," I said. "Coke, Fanta or a strange looking local soft drink?"

The door opened, Deniz's head and shoulders appearing in the crack at the top of the door.

"No way! Is this place alcohol free?"

"Looks that way," I said, shaking two mini cans of cola in her direction.

"Yok artık!" she said, rolling her eyes. "Is there tea?"

I peered around the old-fashioned TV set on the desk. "Yep."

"Tea for me then. Two sugars. *No milk*, you hear me, Englishman?"

"Black tea, coming up."

I boiled the kettle and prepared two cups, carrying them over to the small lounge area with the sofa and placing them on the table. Moments later, Deniz left the bathroom wrapped in a towel, her trousers folded in her hands, and climbed into the huge bed. She pulled the covers up to her shoulders.

"I'll bring yours over," I said, standing.

"Bring yours, too," she said.

I felt myself blush and angled my eyes downward.

"Well, I'm not shouting across the room to you."

"Fair point," I said and carried the two cups over, handing Deniz's to her and placing my own on the bedside table. My cargo pants were filthy with dust. "If I'm going to sit in the bed with you, I should probably—"

"Take them off. Yep."

I unfastened my trousers and slid them to the ground, then turned to climb under the covers. Deniz was naked, her wild curls just barely covering her breasts.

"Hi," she said.

"Hello," I replied. She leaned in and kissed me. Instinct took over and I pulled off my T-shirt and took her in my arms, my hands following the contours of her body as we kissed hungrily, the only occasional pauses coming as she groaned when I accidentally happened upon one of the many bruises from her collision with the thief. We made love, then drifted to sleep, my body coiled around hers.

***

Somehow, I slept right through Deniz waking up, freeing herself from my arms and showering.

"Morning," I said, leaning on one elbow and grinning involuntarily.

"It's alive!" She sauntered from the bathroom, still tying up one of her thick braids and planted a kiss on my lips.

"What time's the meeting again?"

"Eleven. You've got just shy of two hours. But that includes breakfast, so *move*!" She wrenched the covers away.

Blushing ludicrously as I was reminded of my nakedness, I covered my modesty and dashed for the shower.

***

After munching our way through a breakfast of boiled eggs, olives, fuul—a type of bean stew that's better than it sounds— and some flatbread that Deniz revealed translated literally to 'the food of the land' in the Egyptian Arabic dialect, we were back on the street. The sun was intensely hot for ten thirty in the morning, but I supposed that was to be expected. The pavements were fairly quiet, many folk already at their places of work, while the road was a seemingly-endless tailback of clapped-out old cars, none worse than the taxis, many of which were missing windows and entire panels of bodywork.

The constant honking of horns was maddening, but I tried to tune it out by focussing on the peculiarities of the street. Corn cobs grilling in their thousands, cruise boats jostling for position along the Nile, and the blend of ancient minarets and gleaming glass towers making for an even more impressive skyline in the daylight.

"We're here," said Deniz, grabbing my arm and darting onto a pedestrian crossing with a remarkable momentary absence of traffic. The university was a colonial building, standing proud among neatly trimmed patches of grass. The upper parts were decorated with corniches which seemed to have come through the 2011 uprising unscathed.

In the reception area Deniz did the talking, her Arabic fluid and confident. We were directed to the first floor and a classic university corridor of panelled wooden doors and laminate flooring in a ghastly shade of green. We approached the fourth door on the right, inscribed with 'Dr. Hossam Mansour,' and knocked.

"Come," said a deep voice from inside. A short, heavyset man with a bald head was peering suspiciously over his glasses, until he recognised Deniz. His features softened into a grin, and he was quickly on his feet. "Mashallah, it is *so* good to see you, Deniz!" He kissed her on the cheek, then turned to me. "And you must be ..."

"Seb," I said. "A ... friend of Deniz."

"A bit more than a friend," she said and locked her fingers into mine.

"Great! Wonderful!" he said and ushered us into the seats in front of his desk, before taking his own. "Would you like coffee? I'll get coffee." He buzzed the departmental assistant to bring coffees and cream, before splaying his hands on the desk in front of him and letting out a satisfied sigh. "So, the Mamluk martyr? What's your interest in it? It's far from canonical scripture."

Deniz looked at me, gulping in breath, then paused before she spoke. "Do you want the version that will make you think I'm insane or the sanitised, academically appropriate one?"

Dr. Mansour arched one of his eyebrows curiously. "Having seen only the tiniest glimpse of crazy Deniz when we were studying in the states, I'm leaning toward the first option."

"Promise not to call security?"

Mansour placed his hand on his heart and nodded.

We took turns explaining everything that had happened from the first, confusing moments in Anatolia, through Tunisia and our meeting with Kalifi, to Oz's disappearance and our encounter with the bag-snatcher the night before. At every stage, our recounting of the tale became more panicked and frenetic. By the time we reached the breathless end, Mansour's complexion was significantly paler.

"Wh-where's that coffee?" he said, then buzzed back through to the assistant.

A dishevelled young man of eighteen or so shuffled into the office moments later with three mugs, arranged around a steaming coffee pot and a small jug. He glanced at our intense faces and seemingly thought better of speaking before quickly leaving. Mansour's brow was tightly knitted as he poured the almost-black liquid into the cups, as though deep in concentration.

I added some cream from the jug and took a mug, feeling the warmth diffusing into my hands, in contrast to the fierce air-conditioning unit blasting cold air from above Mansour's shiny head.

"I lost my faith a long, *long* time ago," he said, his eyes glazed over, as if somewhere else. "That's not to say I believe in nothing. But a god watching over us, in the traditional sense … it's hard to reconcile. Especially having been here in Cairo the last ten years."

"That's not difficult to understand," said Deniz, stirring a cube of sugar into her cup. "But I can assure you, this is not some collective hallucination. Nor coincidence. When this idiot first emailed me about the curse, I almost told him to find a fortune teller or something. But when he told me *which* curse it was, well, my interest was piqued."

"Of course. And I'm not doubting anything you've told me. There's too much there for it to all have been a series of coincidences."

"So, can you help us?"

"I think so." He stood and moved over to a table at the back of the office where there were a number of old books, bound in ancient leather and vellum, alongside some strips of parchment. All were tightly wrapped in plastic coating, to shield their fragile pages from the environment. He put on a pair of surgical gloves, then began to uncover one of the bound texts, before carrying it over to the main desk.

He cleared the coffee tray to one side and gingerly opened the book to a page toward the end of the volume, marked with a gilt-edged fabric bookmark.

"As with all the saints, it's hard to know sometimes what is truth and what is embellishment. Sometimes the theology, or even just writing a more compelling story takes precedence. I don't need to tell you that." He smiled warmly at Deniz. "But anyway, this is my best guess."

He carefully turned the tome to face us. The page was made up of quadrants of calligraphy in faintly metallic ink and a small diagram in the bottom left corner, which appeared to be a crude sort of map. He placed his finger over a symbol which looked like a crown, with minute Arabic script underneath.

"This is the mausoleum of the first shaykh to introduce Sufism to Mamluk Egypt. It's one of the oldest tombs which still exists in the old necropolis. The tomb most commonly mentioned in the stories of the Mamluk saint you are looking for is almost directly opposite. From the main portal, seen on the old map, here, you must follow the road to its end. Here, on the left side is the tomb of a favourite wife of one of the early Mamluk rulers. You'll recognise it from details in jade on the exterior wall. On the right is the tomb I believe you are looking for."

Deniz took out her phone and took a photo of the map.

"Thank you, Hossam. This is the only lead we have."

"But I must warn you of something—"

"If it's the people living in the city of the dead, Deniz has already told me. We'll be in and out as quickly as possible and before sunset," I said.

"No, no, that I had assumed you would be aware of. It's simply that, last night, before closing, a man came to the general collections and took out the other copy of this text, along with several others on the topic. I asked Hassan, who brought us the coffee, for his details, but it seems he didn't speak Arabic, almost at all. Just showed him a piece of paper with the name of the saint and—"

"Oz! We have to go. Now." Deniz stood, leaned in to Dr. Mansour and kissed him on the cheek. "I shall buy you dinner, Hossam, before we leave. Thank you for this."

"Yes, thank you so much," I added.

"Tell me when you find your friend, please. And if you need anything more …"

"Thank you, Doctor."

We paced the length of the corridor and down the stairs to the main exit, Deniz several steps ahead of me. She stalked over to the roadside and held out an arm for a taxi.

"Al Maqbara," she said as we sat.

The necropolis.

# Chapter Fifteen

I'd never get used to Egyptian driving. We careened up the main street straddling the west bank of the Nile then onto the city ring road, the driver using the horn where I might have gone for the brake. We swerved in and out of the dense traffic, all while I fought against the g-force, reaching out for something to hold onto and mostly finding missing panels, with random pieces of metal jutting out threateningly, as if in some medieval torture device.

As the highway rose to the north of the city, the medieval citadel came into view, the towering minarets and broad, squat domes of the Muhammad Ali Mosque dominating the skyline. Unlike the simple, monolithic sixth-century architecture of the Uqba back in Tunisia, this was intricate, garnished with fine details in the brickwork, domes of gleaming, pearlescent white, reflecting the scorching sun. I forgot about righting myself in the back of the clapped-out old taxi and marvelled at it.

Moments later we were rolling down an exit ramp, the endless blue of the sky devoured by the greying sandstone of buildings from another age, tightly packed along narrow streets. After several more questionable manoeuvres, the driver pulled up and hit the button on the meter. I delved into my wallet for a wad of crinkled notes and handed them over, before jumping out and joining Deniz on the street. She held her phone in front of her, eyes fixed firmly on the map she'd photographed in Mansour's office.

She lifted her gaze and silently mouthed the words on the entry gate to the necropolis.

"This is it," she said and entered. I followed close behind. "This is the first tomb Hossam mentioned. The shaykh. See how the brick is of a different form from the newer buildings?"

I moved closer, trying to perceive the difference, but struggled in the limited light.

"I'm not sure, to be honest. But I believe you. So, from here, it's straight to the other end of the street, right?"

Deniz nodded and moved down the road.

Nothing stirred, the sounds of the bustling citadel beyond the cemetery walls quietening to a low hum. My shoes scuffed noisily on the uneven slabs of the path.

"Seb, look, jade." Deniz pointed toward a calligraphic frieze on the left-hand wall at the end of the road. I squinted to make it out, but it was too far away. Deniz broke into a jog and I picked up my own pace.

"It's the one he mentioned. The king's favourite wife." She traced her fingers along the plaque of symbols, the precious stone glowing, seemingly illuminated from within.

"Which means ..." I turned to the other end of the street and my heart plunged into my gut. The dull, metallic door on the mausoleum we presumed belonged to the saint had been wrenched from its hinges. It lay against the wall, the metal warped. "No! No, no, no." I dashed to the tomb and stepped into the doorway.

Inside, there was a simple sarcophagus, fashioned from heavy stone. The lid had been prised open and pushed backward at an angle. A crowbar, twisted in the effort, lay on the dusty ground.

"The curse fabric?" said Deniz, standing behind me. I edged forward and peered inside the sarcophagus. The body lay there—now no more than a skeleton—wrapped in a simple shroud, much of which had been eaten away by time. A gold charm necklace with calligraphy across a stone of deep red was placed around the neck of the body, while gripped in one of the hands was a thin metal tube.

I gingerly pulled it away from the bony fingers and looked inside.

Empty.

"Fuck!" I shouted and launched the tube against the wall, where it bounced off with a clang. "You think it was Oz?"

"Who else? You heard what Hossam said at the—wait. Do you hear that?"

"What?" I turned my head toward the entrance to the mausoleum. I could hear raised voices. Footsteps.

"We should get out of here."

We hurried out of the mausoleum and into the shadows of the narrow street in front. A group of around a dozen people were shambling toward us from the far end of the path, led by a woman in tattered clothes, whose age might just as easily have been forty or eighty. Her mouth was agape as she yelled words which, I could tell, were not kind.

"What's she saying?"

Deniz scrunched her eyes half shut, listening intently. "It's hard to make out. A lot of colloquialism in there. But I definitely heard 'grave robbers.' Like I said, we need to get out of here."

They were blocking the whole path, so we spun on our heels and darted up the road the way we'd come into the necropolis. As we were about halfway to the gate, two older men and a teenage boy squeezed through it. The men were each holding fragments of sandstone bricks. The man closest to us hefted his chunk of stone in his hand, then shouted something at us before launching the rock. I instinctively flinched away and it smashed into my back, near my shoulder.

I staggered forward, almost falling to the ground, but managed to right myself. I turned back to find another hunk of rock fly past my head by a matter of inches.

"Are they with the others?"

"They're using similar words, so I guess so."

"The other path, left, beside the king's wife's tomb. Shall we try it?"

"It leads deeper into the cemetery complex, but maybe we can lose these thugs and find another way out."

I reached out for Deniz's hand without thinking and pulled her down the path. The noise of the other group was louder now; they'd almost reached the main path by the time we got to the end. We sprinted round the corner, trying not to choke in the sandy dust kicked up as our feet slapped against the stone.

The road narrowed, forcing us to slow our pace and move into single file. I hugged the wall and gestured for Deniz to go in front.

"If they throw more rocks—"

Deniz cut me off: "They'll hit you instead of me. Is that a *good* thing?"

"Let's say it's a *less bad* thing. Keep moving."

She eyed me harshly, twisting her mouth into a grimace, but pressed on, regardless.

The narrow path opened out into a small square. Two pairs of large tombs with marble façades faced one another either side of a large fig tree, with only a fraction of its fruit remaining. We stopped for breath as we scoped out the exits. I rotated my left arm, the shoulder still smarting from the hit with the stone. The path opposite the one we'd entered from was a dead end, so that was out. To our right, the narrow road was littered with debris from a collapsed mausoleum wall just a few metres in. The path to our left was wide open, the flickering light from a burning lamp beckoning to us.

The sound of the rabble interrupted the quiet in the courtyard, songbirds fleeing in all directions from the gnarled branches of the fig tree. Our eyes met and we each understood. We took a breath and charged into the broad street to our left.

"Look! Up ahead," I said between breaths. "There's a gate."

"I see it. Try to keep it in sight."

We reached the end of the wide road, which formed a T-junction. The path to the right was clear. I turned back to the check the path left and, as I did, a rock smashed into Deniz's temple. She crumpled to the ground, the back of her head smashing into the stone.

A wave of cold rushed over my body and I covered my mouth with my hands. Another group of people in filthy, ragged clothing were ambling toward us, chanting something unpleasant. I crouched beside Deniz and was relieved to find she was still breathing. The gash at her temple was already swelling and when I felt the back of her head, her hair was slick with blood.

I stood and shielded her from the crowd, just as the first two groups appeared at the end of the road. I raised my hands in surrender.

"We didn't take anything. I'm sorry. We didn't break in. Please. My friend is hurt."

The two groups stopped and whispered amongst themselves.

"I don't speak Arabic. I need to get my friend to a hospit—"

"Show bag!" the old woman from the first group said through broken teeth. She reached out with a claw-like hand.

"Okay. Okay," I said and lowered my hands, slowly sliding the shoulder bag from Deniz's motionless body. I unfastened the catches and opened it, showing the tablet, wallet and notebook inside. "We didn't take anything. Please let me take my friend to the hospital." I spoke slowly, enunciating every syllable as clearly as I could, keeping one eye on Deniz for any signs of movement.

"What you look for?"

"There was nothing there. The sarco—the grave was empty."

"What you *look* for?"

I ignored the question and crouched to check on Deniz. The old woman spat something in harsh Arabic across to one of the older men in the second group of cemetery-dwellers. He tilted his head one way then the other, before lumbering toward me, hands slightly raised and balled into bony fists.

"Stay away," I shouted.

He flinched, but advanced further. He reached in and swiped Deniz's bag from me. I tried to hold on, but I was on my haunches, off balance. He rifled through her things and, having realised we'd taken nothing, lifted out her leather wallet.

"Put that back," I yelled and got to my feet, knocking the wallet from his hands and onto the ground. His expression soured as he seemed to process what I'd done while so mightily outnumbered. He reached out with both hands and grabbed my neck. He squeezed and I felt my eyes bulge in their sockets. I wrapped my hands around his and tried to prise him off, but he was too strong.

My vision blurred, black spots moving in and out of focus at the edges of my line of sight. Knowing I was about to faint and dreading what might come next, I searched the faces of the crowd, all of them watching on, clearly unperturbed by what was happening.

"Stop!" A long, protracted bellow from off to the left.

The man's grip relaxed, and I shoved him backward before bending double, coughing and gasping for air.

"*I* robbed the grave."

I recognised the voice now: Oz.

"This is what I was looking for." He held up a long strip of fabric which matched the end we'd happened upon—which had been left to taunt us, in all likelihood—in the museum in Tunis. He stood halfway up a collapsed tomb wall, holding out the material in front of him in one hand, rucksack slung over his shoulder. "Let my friend go, and I return it to you. You can do what you want with me."

"Oz, no!" I shouted across to him.

"Deniz needs a hospital. You must go."

"And what about you? We came to find you—to stop you from—"

"There's no other way, Seb. Kalifi said it. You heard him."

"This ... there has to be another way."

He shook his head, then gestured to the angry mob, who had moved to one side to create an exit tunnel for me.

"These people could kill you, Oz." My eyes were wet now, my voice fractured.

He shrugged. "I've made peace with death. And we both know *he* wants me alive."

"He?"

His eyes flicked to the curse fabric.

"You have the name?"

He nodded.

"Don't do it. Oz, don't!"

"Go. You're wasting time. Deniz could ..." He trailed off.

I knew he was right. I stuffed Deniz's wallet back into her bag, then crouched and lifted her into a fireman's carry. As I made to leave the courtyard, I paused at the exit, and turned.

"We're at the Safir Hotel. Find us. We'll help you. We'll think of something."

"You know I won't. Now *go!*"

I edged through the crowd, the people jostling to occupy the space after I passed, like sand squeezing through the waist of an hourglass. As I reached the road, I opened the door of the first taxi I saw and laid Deniz on the back seat. A roar sounded from behind me, and I tried not to think what they might have done. I climbed into the front passenger seat.

"Hospital, fast."

# Chapter Sixteen

Deniz came round as the battered chassis of the ancient cab rattled over a bumpy stretch of road. I did my best to calm her as the driver whisked us to a private hospital, close to the centre.

She was checked over and given a quick x-ray, which determined there'd mercifully been no fracture to the skull, and discharged with strict instructions for twenty-four hours' rest and for me to be wary of concussion symptoms. Another taxi, this one slightly less antiquated, chauffeured us back to the Safir. We made our way to the room and Deniz got settled in bed, while I went back down to reception to order some soup from room service.

I tried Oz's phone for the thousandth time while I waited in line. Predictably, straight to voicemail.

"Listen, mate … I hope you got away from that mob earlier. Please … please think about coming to talk to us. We're at the Safir. I told you already. There has to be—there *is*—another way, I know it in my gut. We can work it out together. Call me anytime. See you soon, Oz." I slipped my phone away and paid for the food before heading back upstairs.

Deniz was sitting up in bed when I entered the room, chatting loudly in Arabic on the phone. I shook my head, worried, and sat on the sofa in one corner of the room, watching her animatedly gesturing with her free hand—something she curiously did far more in Arabic than either English or her native Turkish.

"What are you doing?" I said, the moment she hung up.

"That was the other expert I told you about before we came across to Egypt. She's coming over."

"You're supposed to be resting!" I leapt to my feet, my head swimming with the sudden movement. Deniz was quiet while she stashed her phone away in her bag on the bedside table.

"I heard the doctor, loud and clear. But Oz doesn't have time for me to follow doctor's orders."

"Let me take more of the burden."

"Dr Ikram doesn't speak much English. You need me on this. I told her about the necropolis, so she said she'd come here. She's bringing some documents over."

I scrunched my face up, frustrated that I could do nothing but agree to her plans.

"When's she going to be here?"

"Half an hour."

***

We'd just finished our room service soup, Deniz feeling well enough to get out of bed and throw some clothes on, when the buzzer sounded. We made our introductions, but it was clear Ikram's English was every bit as limited as Deniz had intimated. I left them to their discussion and went out for a walk upriver toward the north of the city.

I was conscious of my heightened nerves after the robbery the previous day, searching the faces of everyone I passed, scrutinising them for hostile intentions. Apart from a few returned glares, no one seemed particularly interested in me.

I crossed the bridge onto Zamalek Island and passed the ornate fountain in front of the opera house and the many gardens around it, before moving onto the next bridge over to the east bank. Once across the river, I strolled by the sprawling red-brick edifice of the Egyptian museum, its many sphinxes staring out in all directions at the myriad roads around it. Something drove me on from there and, as I passed the building to the north, I felt as though I was being drawn along the main road toward the chaos of the central Ramses train station.

Hawkers crowded the place, selling grilled corn, kebabs, tea, and semi-legally procured train tickets. I did my best to ignore them, weaving in and out of the throng toward the fortress-like station itself. I stood outside and stared up at the building, intricately carved marble details surrounding its stylised Arabic gates and windows. I'd never set foot in that place, yet something stirred in me. Something like déjà vu. A need to hold my eyes wide and take it all in.

My phone buzzed in my pocket and the breath I'd been absent-mindedly holding poured from my lungs.

"Hey, how was it?" I could hear Deniz smiling at the other end of the phone.

"She's got something. Several somethings. Some ideas about how Oz is planning to ..."

"Okay."

"And something else. Something much better. Another way to kill this thing."

"Seriously?"

"Mm-hmm. It's old. Way older than our saint's tale. Pre-Islam. Come back to the hotel, I'll explain."

"Sure. Be about fifteen minutes."

"Where are you?"

"The railway station."

"Thinking of taking off?" Her voice was slathered with playful sarcasm.

"Obviously not. I just felt ... *led* here."

"Someone in the crowd? Oz?"

"Nobody. It's weird. Just looking at the building from here in front. I feel ..."

"Go on."

"I don't know. Doesn't matter, I suppose. I'll see you in fifteen, okay?"

"Meet me in the coffee bar. I feel like a decent cup."

***

As I entered the café, Deniz was sitting in a booth, swiping at the screen of her tablet.

"What are you having?" I said, hovering.

"I just ordered us both cardamom coffees. Sit."

I did as I was told. "So …" She clicked the button on the side of the tablet, putting it to sleep. "Doctor Ikram was brilliant. She thinks she has an alternative. Do you remember when we landed in Tunis, there was a shadow over Oz, from a cloud?"

"Yeah, a wild dog or something?"

"Almost. A hyena."

"Okay."

An immaculately dressed waitress arrived and placed two coffees in front of us, alongside a bowl of brown sugar cubes. "Anything else?" she asked, beaming.

"Lah, shukran," Deniz said and waved her away with a small tip. "Anyway, I told you at the time, the *true* form of the djinn in the purely physical realm is the hyena. Or something like it. At least in this part of the world. There's some conjecture in Oman, as well as east of Saudi, but I digress. Ikram brought me over a couple cases from folklore of the djinn being killed while in animal form."

"So, we get the djinn to possess an animal. Is this *that* different to what Oz is trying?"

"No, that's the thing. They don't need to possess anything. To all intents and purposes, they *are* that animal. The only way they can appear here in our material world, without hijacking someone else, is as that animal."

I scratched the stubble on my chin as I thought about it, then took a sip of my coffee. "Okay, but if this change is wilful, how are we going to convince this powerful, malevolent thing to turn into a hyena on command, never mind stay in that form while we shoot it or whatever?"

"That's where the stories come in." She swiped her tablet to life and turned it to face me. A scan of an antiquated looking illustration was emblazoned across the screen, floating scrolls of calligraphy dotting the scene. "This is a story from an epic poet in Syria, about one thousand three hundred years old. See, this guy—the shaman—commands the djinn into its original form and then binds it to sleep. Then this warrior guard, whose mistress—a queen of some small kingdom that doesn't exist anymore—has been harassed by the djinn for years, takes out his scimitar and cuts the things head off. Poof, no more djinn."

I couldn't help but laugh at the simple way in which Deniz told the story.

"What's the catch?"

"What catch?"

"There's *always* a catch."

She turned the tablet so it was face down on the table and drained her coffee cup.

"We still need the name."

"Which Oz has?"

She nodded vigorously. "And Ikram knew our saint's story. Knew of the curse. But she's convinced that the djinn involved has never had his name written anywhere else. People were too afraid."

I thumped my fist down onto the table. "Isn't there an official list of all the djinn somewhere, for fuck's sake?"

The murmur of the café died down to silence and every pair of eyes in the room locked onto me.

"Sorry," I said, hands raised, open in apology.

"Doctor Ikram also had some advice for tracking Oz down. She said that he'll likely be contacting fortune tellers. A lot of them produce flyers, handing them out at the bus station, or wherever, promising to solve all your problems—money, love—"

"The usual bullshit."

"Exactly. But also, communication with the djinn."

"Obviously bullshit, too."

"It is, and that's what she said. Which buys us a little time. Oz will be going through these people, trying to find out if any of them are the real deal. He can't summon the djinn into himself alone. Not without guidance on the right words, not to mention pronunciation. His Arabic is pretty miserable, remember?"

"True."

"But Ikram has given me the mobile number of someone she thinks might actually *be* the real deal."

"Who is it?"

"An eleven-year-old boy called Mohammad."

"Are you fucking serious?"

"Deadly. Ikram did some work with him last year, after he claimed he had a 'pet' djinn who helped him find treasure from the ancient Egyptian period."

I half-laughed, half-choked at the ridiculous suggestion. "This is beyond stupid."

"He's found statuettes, precious stones and other stashes worth eighty thousand dollars since he was eight. He's bought a house for his parents and another for his older sister who is at medical school."

"Christ!"

"Not quite, but it's worth checking out."

I blew out air. "We've got nothing else."

# CHAPTER SEVENTEEN

We took the metro out to the run-down residential district of Ezbet El-Nakhl after a quick but promising phone conversation with young Mohammad. He'd agreed to meet us at the communal football pitch where he usually met clients looking for his help.

As we exited the metro station, the scene was a world away from downtown Cairo, with its five-star hotels and designer boutiques. Houses and apartment blocks were built almost on top of one another and existed in states of incompletion or near-collapse.

A brilliant blue dome from the area's grand mosque gleamed like a jewel in an otherwise grimly dull skyline. We traipsed the gridded streets, between row after row of tightly packed houses, women and children sitting in play on doorsteps, veils over faces as much to protect them from the swirling clouds of dust as for anything related to modesty.

Beyond something which was either a car park or a graveyard for ancient-looking buses, we spotted the football pitch. Black-and-white-striped, handmade goalposts played host to young boys, cupping their hands around their mouths to scream instructions at their teammates.

Just along from the shabbily dressed players sat a tall, thin boy whose clothes looked newer than those of the others. He seemed not to be paying attention to the game.

Rather, he watched a group of sparrows as they hared from trees to balconies in search of scraps.

"Mohammad?" I said enquiringly as we approached from behind.

"Seb, yes?"

Only Deniz had spoken to him on the phone, without mentioning my name. The first of many strange events in the young boy's presence. He turned to face us, standing and outstretching a gangly hand toward me in a way that was curiously adult for a boy not yet in his teenage years. "I asked about you. They told me your story checked out. Would you like some tea?"

Deniz and I eyed one another, then accepted his offer. He stood, barked an instruction to one of the aspiring footballers while pointing to his plastic chair, then led us to the corner and a small café. The inside was thick with shisha smoke, a group of men sitting around a large table smoking and drinking tea or coffee. They ignored us as we waited outside, and Mohammad entered to order for us.

"Sit," he said, gesturing to a round table with a chessboard in its centre. "They will bring for us."

We sat, and a silence descended until a man with a toothless but friendly smile brought out three glass teacups on a tray. He laid our drinks in front of us, and a sugar pot in the middle, before disappearing back inside.

"So, your friend. He is in trouble?"

I explained what had happened up to that point, trying to give as much detail as possible, Deniz occasionally chiming in in Arabic to provide more, particularly in the matter of the curse and the alternative measures Doctor Ikram had laid out the day before.

"My friends say you are telling the truth. And that your friend hasn't yet found anyone to help him call on the djinn who is following him. They also say they can give you a prayer or a mantra to turn the djinn into his animal form."

I sat forward in my chair, narrowing my eyes. "They're with you now?"

The boy laughed playfully, betraying his tender age. "Always they are with me. But you won't see. They are of fire and air. Seen when they will it."

Deniz nodded in confirmation.

"What do we have to do? Should we pay you?" I asked.

Again he laughed, throwing his head back this time. When he stopped, he locked me with a hard stare. "You must help me find the next treasure."

At first, I chuckled, certain this was a wind up—a joke at the expense of the uninitiated foreigner. But he held his expression, firmly focussed, not even a hint of a smile.

"Your friend told you, it's what we do. They tell me where to find treasure and I dig."

"She told me. But why do you live in this dump if you've found so much treasure?"

"*They* live here, so I stay close."

I shook my head, incredulous. But nothing about the last two weeks made any sense to me. I listened to my own voice, as though I were an observer, outside my own body, as I agreed to meet him the next morning on the east bank of the Nile, south of Helwan.

***

The sun was barely peeking over the eastern horizon when we stepped down from the service taxi. It was a battered, narrow Daihatsu van, somehow fitted with nine seats, in addition to the driver. Two older women moved to allow my 'wife' and I to sit together, mercifully.

The spot where Mohammad had asked to meet us was desolate. A petrol station with a small café sat at the side of the road, while some old, apparently disused warehouses occupied the west bank of the river.

"Where could anyone possibly have hidden treasure *here?*" I said after a few moments.

"I was wondering the same thing," Deniz said, holding her cardigan tight to her body against the chill of the morning.

"He should know." I nodded to the two shadows moving toward us from the petrol station.

"My friends, you found the spot," Mohammad called. The figure at his side towered over him, as well as being at least twice as wide. "This my uncle, Brahim. My driver."

I stepped forward as they got closer, extending my hand toward the uncle. "Seb," I said. He mumbled, wiped his hand on his robe then clasped mine.

"He doesn't speak English." Mohammad grinned.

"What are we doing here?" I asked, looking about me to emphasise the emptiness of the place.

"The island," Mohammad said, pointing over my shoulder. "My friends say there is gold there."

The 'island' Mohammad was talking about was a dark patch of silty land, reeds and grasses sprouting from it at a variety of angles. It was at least three or four metres from the eastern shore where we stood.

"How do we get to it?"

"Boat is coming."

I looked at Deniz, who shrugged, eyes wide. I was about to enquire further when Mohammad spoke again.

"Boat. Look!"

Coming upriver from the direction of the Cairene suburb of Helwan was the most dilapidated felucca I have ever seen. Its sail was torn in several places, while the wood of the hull was dotted with splits and stained with rot. The pilot didn't look to be in much better condition. My concern only grew when he insisted on taking us over to the island no more than two at a time.

Mohammad and Brahim took the first trip, the older man hauling a small bag of tools. The boatman picked up a pole from the deck that was slightly thinner than his frail arms and punted across. We took the second trip, then watched as the boatman tied up the felucca on the riverbank and took out a pack of cigarettes, along with a small camping stove on which he placed a teapot.

I turned back to Mohammad. "Where do your 'friends' say the treasure is?" I made air quotes as I said 'friends' and got an elbow in the back from Deniz. "Sorry. What do they say?"

"We have to dig. This place. Here." He moved over to a spot on the edge of the small islet, bare of vegetation.

"And what are we looking for?"

"Gold? Stones? I never know until we find it." He smiled broadly. "But we always find something. Come on." He handed me a mattock and Deniz a small trowel.

"Don't you have anything more substantial?" she protested.

Mohammad shrugged and reached into the bag for a shovel.

Brahim stood beside the boatman, smoking while we worked. Some thirty minutes into the dig, Deniz hit something.

"Seb, bring that over here."

I hurried over with my mattock and chipped away at the firmer soil at the base of the narrow trench Deniz had dug. Something shimmered within the near-black mud.

"Carefully," said Mohammad and elbowed me aside. He stepped down into the ditch and scrabbled away the soil with his fingers, before pulling out a golden disc and a small boat, also seemingly fashioned from gold.

"Is that—"

"Ancient. I think yes," he said, grinning as he lightly dusted particles of mud from the thin grooves in the boat's hull.

We took turns trawling through the disturbed earth and came up with several gemstones set in gilt surrounds and a number of polished semiprecious stones. Only when Mohammad—and his friends, of course—were satisfied the earth had given up everything it had been hiding did he whistle for the boatman.

Deniz and I made the short crossing first, this time carrying the tool bag, while the others came on the second, with the treasure haul placed delicately into a cloth satchel.

"Thank you for your help. Now I ask my friends to help you." He turned to his left and spoke in short bursts in Arabic. He gestured, threw up his hands and varied his tone as though having a normal conversation, though the space in front of him was a void. My rational self wanted to reject him as a charlatan. A fortune teller who'd found his gift for peddling lies to people too young. But I'd helped dig up that treasure, not to mention the maddening things I had seen since that ice cream cart had been moved into the morning light and set off this whole process.

I would wait, and quieten my sceptical nature, for Oz.

"My friends," he said finally. "Özgur has found one like me. A woman. Older. He has what he needs."

"What? But you said—" I was on my feet before I even realised.

"When I said, it was true. This morning he found her. She asked him for a lot of money."

"And what now? Where will he go to ..." I couldn't vocalise it.

"My friends tell me you know the answer. You were there and you felt it."

"Ramses."

Deniz tugged at my arm. "What?"

"The station. I felt something when I was there. We have to go." I strode on toward the petrol station, taking out my phone to arrange a taxi.

"Wait," the boy called out to me.

I spun to face him.

"I need to give you the commands."

Deniz rushed forward, taking her notepad from her shoulder bag and handing it to him. Mohammad grasped the pen and wrote quickly, his handwriting surprisingly elegant, looping from right to left on the page. She began to mouth the words and Mohammad held up a hand.

"Not now. Only when you are ready."

Deniz nodded and stuffed the notebook back inside.

"Thank you," I called.

"Good luck. Inshallah, you reach Özgur in time."

# Chapter Eighteen

The Uber that turned up to meet us was a Nissan Primera in surprisingly roadworthy condition. The driver, Yusuf, sped off almost as soon as we sat down.

"What time your train?" he said as we rolled up the ramp onto the riverside highway.

Deniz and I stumbled over our words for a moment.

"No train. We're meeting a friend. He's there now," she said, finally.

"Oh no!" the driver said, wagging his finger in the air. "Ramses far. One hour and half."

"I understand," I said. "Just as fast as possible, please."

"Yes, sir," he said with a flick of his head, accelerating.

I sat back in my seat and closed my eyes, focusing on keeping my breathing even as the panic brought on by the sense of utter powerlessness rose in my chest. I felt a nudge in my ribs and my eyes flicked open.

"Do you see that?" Deniz grasped my hand in hers and pointed between the front head rests. A cloud so black it seemed to suck the light from the remainder of the sky was spreading over the capital, its tendrils unfurling down the road toward us. "He knows we're coming."

"I just hope we're not too late."

***

Thirty minutes into our journey, the heavens opened. The kind of rain that dropped like bombs onto the roof of the car above our heads. As it thrashed down, the road surface's limited drainage capacity was soon overcome, the highway coated with a layer of standing water, shimmering with oil ingrained into the tarmac over many searing dry months.

"I have to drive more slow, sorry sir," the driver said, his hands tightly gripping the wheel.

Older, poorly equipped cars slid across the road as it curved gently to the left, hugging the bank of the Nile. I squeezed Deniz's hand. She squeezed back.

Our taxi lost traction, sliding toward the riverside barrier, then the driver's jaw tensed as he steered into the turn while gently accelerating until the tyres found grip once more and pulled us into the centre of the carriageway.

"Sorry," I said as I loosened my too-tight grip on Deniz's hand.

She smiled. "It's okay. Try to relax. The driver has everything under control. We're going to make it."

As she spoke, a shadow covered her face. I flicked my head toward the front windscreen just in time to see the colossal, barrel-rolling form of a black Skoda SUV from the other side of the road slam down onto its roof, on top of a pair of ancient Peugeot taxis. It bounced from the boxy roofs, before thumping down onto the road and sliding toward us, a shower of sparks spewing from either side of the vehicle as it squealed along the road.

Our driver stamped down on the brakes, twisting the wheel one way and the other. The car refused to respond.

"Hold on!" I managed over the ear-splitting noise.

The black-and-silver grille of the vehicle loomed large in the front window. I braced myself for impact, scrunching my eyes closed. We stopped dead. I peeled my eyes open.

"Are you okay?" I said when my head had stopped spinning.

The door beside Deniz had buckled inward but, though she looked shaken, she seemed unhurt.

"Deniz?"

She raised a hand to her head and rubbed her temple. "Things *really* have to stop hitting me in the head."

"Are you cut?" I leaned in to check, brushing aside her hair.

"I don't think so. At least it was the other side from before."

I leaned forward toward the driver, just as sirens began to wail from behind us. "Is there any way for us to keep going? My friend is … in trouble."

"Inshallah the engine starts," he said and turned the key. The car protested a couple of times before roaring to life. He gingerly put it into gear and rolled around the crumpled body of the Skoda. The driver had crawled from the driver's window and, despite the lacerations to his face and hands, was bellowing into his mobile phone in the still pouring rain.

Yusuf veered onto the hard shoulder and switched on his hazard lights. We were back on our way.

***

The driver looked every bit as relieved as I felt as we pulled up across the road from Ramses. The rain was still cascading down in a near endless torrent from the pitch-dark sky. I dashed from the car, Deniz following close behind. We skittered through puddles dotting the uneven cobblestone square in front of the station and into the building.

Water rolled in through the wide-open doors, smothering the forecourt and rendering the marble floor as slippery as a skating rink.

"What now? Where could Oz be planning …" Deniz trailed off.

I glanced around the space, people huddled together, their clothes and baggage sopping wet. Then a bolt of thunder shook the building.

"Outside."

"In this? Are you sure?"

I shrugged. "I have a feeling. I had it when I walked here the other day. *Before* I walked here even. I can't explain it."

"Good enough for me."

Deniz led the way out of the station and into the driving downpour. The streets were deserted of people, the market sellers all closed. Even the corn and snack vendors had shut for business, tarpaulins draped over their grills and trolleys. Cars were backed up as far as the eye could see, their horns blaring as the traffic stubbornly refused to shift along the waterlogged streets.

"Where did you get the feeling?" she shouted over the thrumming of the rain.

"Right out front." I moved a few steps further forward. About turned to face the main doors. "Here. Only my gaze was pulled … that way." I pointed to my left. A hundred metres or so behind the main building there was a signal gantry over the tracks.

A shadowy figure balanced precariously in the middle, holding onto one of the sets of signal lights.

I tried to speak but managed only a croak as my body trembled uncontrollably. I raised my hand again, pointed toward the figure until Deniz saw what I could see.

"We have to stop him." Deniz grabbed my hand and dragged me around the side of the station. A chicken wire fence ran the length of the track, once the station building ended but, this being the Ramses district, one of Cairo's most crime-ridden areas, someone had already cut holes through, allowing us in.

I snagged my arm on the sharp wire on my way through, tearing the fabric of my T-shirt, but we were soon onto the railway tracks. I called out Oz's name, but he couldn't hear me through the maelstrom. I checked for oncoming trains, then moved toward him as quickly as I could, my feet getting bogged down in puddles of water in depressions in the ballast either side of the rails.

"Oz," Deniz shouted.

This time, he turned.

The green traffic light illuminated his battered and bruised face, highlighting the dark patch around his eye and slashes peeling away from one side of his jaw.

"We've found another way! You don't have to—"

"It's too late, Seb. It's done." He held the coiled curse fabric in his hand.

A lightning bolt slammed into the ground on the other side of a stationary goods train, just beyond the gantry, releasing a deafening explosion of sonic energy.

"What do you mean?" I yelled after the sound had dissipated. "How can it be?"

"Get off the tracks! Move away!" His gaze shot up to the sky, where a pillar of swirling flame had materialised, stretching itself out from the low cloud like a burning butterfly hauling itself from the confines of its chrysalis. He raised both hands above his head and swayed on his feet as the fire descended and coiled itself around him.

"Tell Marie I loved her until the end. Sıla, too. All my family. And you. I love you! Now *get back*!"

Oz's knees gave way and his body twisted as he fell.

"Seb!" Deniz shoved me backward. I looked beyond her to see the single, blinding eye of the train as it charged down the track toward us from the south. I reached my arms around her and hauled us both off the track and onto the uneven ground behind me.

Everything seemed to move in slow motion as Oz's body tumbled from the gantry like a rag doll before the blunt head of the engine slammed into him, smashing him high into the air. His head and the right side of his torso caved in with the initial impact, before his limp form came down on top of the fast-braking train's carriages and slid from the rounded roof edge to the ground.

I lay there for I don't know how long, holding Deniz tight to me as the water seeped through my clothes and, seemingly, my skin. I scrunched my eyes closed as though it would prevent what I had just witnessed from being real. As though if I didn't walk around the now-static locomotive, and see his shattered body for myself, somehow my friend would be okay.

Alive.

The only thought I could muster was that I was as broken as I could ever possibly be. That there was no low lower than this.

Then I felt the rain begin to slow and dared to peel my eyelids away from my eyes. And saw the flames snaking away into the retreating clouds.

# Chapter Nineteen

"You said you would take care of him!" Marie was shrieking down the phone.

And, fuck, who could blame her, I would have been, too. I let her scream. Take it out on me. Every verbal punch she landed felt deserved. Violent catharsis. If she'd been close enough to beat me to death, I'd have let her do it. I'd have *encouraged* her to.

Screeching subsided into sobbing, which eventually gave way to a wavering, cracked vocal tone. I didn't say a word until she was silent. I'd spent the entire afternoon and night in a filthy, smoke-filled questioning room in Cairo's downtown police department before being whisked to the coroner's office to formally identify Oz's mangled body. My body ached. I was battered, chilled to the bone and desperate for sleep, but my mind was a whirling dervish of sorrow and rage and guilt.

"What about Sıla?" I asked finally, in a small, weak voice. "Any change?"

"He didn't tell you?" She made a sound somewhere between laughing and choking. "Fuck."

Silence.

"Marie?"

"She's gone."

I felt bile rolling up from my gullet and forced it back down.

"She's what?"

"I thought Oz would have told you. That must be why he … I tried to call him—" Sobbing overcame her, snatching her words away.

I let her cry it out, silently wiping away my own tears. Deniz sat on the bed opposite, hands covering her mouth and nose, her eyes wide and violently red.

"What happened, Marie? Can you tell me?"

I could hear her trying to catch her breath at the other end of the phone.

"First, she woke up. It was just after lunch. Enes had brought clothes for Ceren to change into—she's barely left Sıla's side since you left. He was there in the room for a moment, and she just sat up. Completely normal. Like nothing had ever happened. Then, she looked at her mum and dad and said: 'the woman with the twisted leg says it's Oz's fault.' After that, she collapsed. Flatlined."

I swallowed hard. Waited.

"The doctors tried to—" She choked on her words and wept again.

"We're bringing him back, Marie. I'm so sorry. I know this will never, *never* be okay. But we're bringing him back. See you soon and take care."

I hung up the phone.

"Tell me I misunderstood," Deniz said through her cupped hands. "Tell me she's—"

"I wish I could." The tears flowed and I allowed them. All the emotion spilled over as I stood. Deniz caught me before I fell, and we held each other because neither one of us could have stood alone.

∗∗∗

The journey back to Turkey was sombre, almost silent. We must have exchanged a dozen words for the duration of those ten hours of flights and transfers. We decided to get a cab to the apartment, neither of us feeling quite ready yet to face Enes or the rest of Oz's family.

As we got out and paid the driver, we saw we wouldn't have a choice in that. Enes was leaning against the wall of the apartment, the tip of his cigarette a searing bright point in the shadows of dusk.

"Hoşgeldiniz," he said, stubbing out his cigarette and pulling first Deniz then me into tight bearhugs.

"Enes, I don't know what to say. I'm so sorry."

He released me, placing his hands on both my shoulders and squeezing. "Okay."

As he looked at me straight on, I could see the deep shadows beneath his eyes, the flesh of his face sallow and withered. The last few weeks had aged him immeasurably and I couldn't be sure that he would regain that youthful look he'd had when I'd first met him earlier in the year.

He turned to Deniz and spoke in Turkish, urgency in his voice as he pulled an envelope from his pocket. I noted Oz's blocky handwriting first, then the Tunis postmark. I listened for his inflection, trying to piece together the conversation, but my Turkish wasn't up to much. I had to wait.

When he finished, Deniz relayed to me what Oz had written in his letter; that he had no regrets beyond what it would do to his parents and to Marie. That, whatever the outcome, he would do it over and over if he thought there was a sliver of a chance of it bringing Sıla back from whatever state she was in. I thought I saw Enes wince as Deniz said his daughter's name.

She went on, explaining how Oz had made clear we had done everything we could to help him. That he never would have received the information he needed without us and that we were blameless in his final course of action. Finally, she explained that his letter instructed Enes to ask us for help, should he still need it. And should we be prepared to give it.

"We can't bring Sıla back now," I said, Deniz relaying my words in Turkish. "We have something that might allow us to get back at this thing. But it could still be dangerous and, from what little knowledge we have, seriously unpredictable."

"There are two reasons we *have to* act." Deniz translated his words. "The first, it took my brother and my baby. And second, we can't let it do this again, to someone else. We have to destroy it."

Deniz and I locked eyes for a long moment before I spoke.

"I understand. We're going to need somewhere quiet. And weapons. If this thing works, it's going to be a physical entity. A physical threat, needing material arms."

"I have what we need on the farm. Machetes, guns, whatever we need. And somewhere remote … I know just the place. You should rest. You both look like ghosts. We'll set out at dawn."

# Chapter Twenty

Enes's pick-up truck bumped and bounced over the long, untended road meandering through the forest from the town. The noisy sounds of the street with its myriad scooters and the hubbub of people milling here and there were soon replaced with near silence, the wind whispering through the treetops as birds skittered in all directions, chirping and squawking over the low growl of the truck's engine.

Sunlight was obscured behind the rocky hills and low mountains while a vaporous mist hung close to the ground, lending the scene an unsettling atmosphere. In the truck, none of us spoke. Most of our equipment was in our bags or on the flatbed of the truck, but I clutched the embroidered fragment of fabric tightly in my hands, as though it might ghost away if left unattended. Beside the gold script emblazoned across the blue material was a single stain of deep rust: Oz's blood.

The canopy thinned, then disappeared entirely, and the sky opened into a dome of deep blue, the last remaining specks of starlight and a fragment of the moon the only things punctuating its otherwise spotless appearance.

"We stop here. Walk," Enes said from up front. He pulled in at the side of the road and got out. By the time I had stepped down from the back of the truck and helped Deniz to the ground, Enes had already slung a rifle, and one of the long cloth bags, over his shoulder. He tossed the other across to me with minimal effort, though I was partially winded as it thumped into my chest. "Come," he said, and we followed.

We walked around a hillock, with a long-shuttered café in front, then up a slope of loose stones, where I stopped to take it in. Enes yelled something in Turkish.

"Welcome to Kayakoy: The Ghost town. Quietest place in Anatolia," Deniz translated.

Dozens of squat buildings dotted the hillside, their whitewashed walls faded to a grey that seemed to meld with the lingering mist. Scrubby bushes invaded them from all angles, hammering home the desertion of the town. It had been a small but functioning place, populated peacefully by Greeks, until the first world war and the subsequent conflict between the Ottomans and their own nation. In 1923 it was hurriedly evacuated, the populace moving to Greece as refugees, despite most of them never having visited the place in their lives. This was the result. A true ghost town, where the classrooms of the school still bore decaying calendars and wall displays.

An eerie place.

A silent place.

As good a place as any to trap a demon of air and fire in its animal form and attempt to destroy it.

We unpacked our things on the eastern face of the hillside to make best of use of the light as the sun rose. Deniz laid out a thick goat's-wool blanket on the ground and began looking over the incantation Mohammad had given her back in Helwan.

"I'm going to need no distractions for this, okay? I haven't done meditative prayer since I was a teenager. You boys go and set up in front of the old church."

"What if it materialises close to you?" My voice was slathered with fear, but I was past trying to hide such things.

"I'll run to you. I'm quick. But I don't think it'll happen that way. Part of the summoning is about visualisation. I'll visualise it in open space." She gestured to a point on the opposite edge of the town where two larger buildings had collapsed in a heap of rubble. "Remember, this thing is incredibly smart. And hyenas are agile. Better to face it in the open."

I heaved one of the bags onto my shoulder and began to move toward the church, then turned back to Deniz.

"Listen, if it works ... go back to the truck. Lock yourself inside."

Deniz narrowed her eyes at me. "Because I'm a woman? Remember who stopped that thief in Cairo, şapşal." Playful, even in moments as dramatic as this.

I chewed down on my lip as a wave of emotion slammed into me. "Because I'm not ready to lose someone else I love this week."

She forced a smile onto her face, but her eye twitched as she tried to hold it. "Go."

Enes and I moved down the hillside and across to the front of the church. The corners of the old wooden doors had been eaten away at by the elements, but the portal remained stubbornly closed.

I unfastened the bags and pulled out a large blade. I tried slashing at the air with it. Enes shook his head and took another, began helping me with technique. Using his legs in a strong, supportive position, he held the machete in both hands and stepped forward as he swung it. Infinitely more controlled than my attempt. Stronger, too.

I imitated his swing, not getting it quite right, but clearly far better than my first effort. He waved me over to some shrubs which had grown up between two houses with caved-in roofs and damaged walls. He drove forward and split the plant in two, then stepped away for me to try.

I cut clean through the plant but misjudged the space. The tip of my blade clanged against the antique brickwork, the material crumbling and a shockwave travelling up the knife through the handle and into my shoulders.

Enes laughed and shook his head.

I glanced up the hillside, to where Deniz was now sat cross-legged, eyes closed. Her lips slowly moved around the words of the prayer Mohammad had given her. The first rays of sunlight crept across her features, bringing her olive skin to vivid life, casting shadows over her strong nose and bringing out the auburn in her dark ringlets. My heart swelled in that moment, despite the grave danger we were all about to be in.

"How long?" Enes said.

I shrugged my shoulders.

He set about refining his technique, cutting through bushes and thickets with increasing effectiveness, before wiping the blade with a cloth from his pocket. I half-watched, while my imagination replayed the moment of Oz's death over and over, trying to find a way we could have intervened.

The wind blew across the abandoned old town, gently at first, leaving leaves and other debris dancing in its wake. Then it became harsher, colder, the whispering of its breath replaced with a low howl. I felt a knot in my stomach and got to my feet with my blade.

It was time.

Twigs and forest litter swirled around the space at the edge of the town, but among the green of pine needles and the brown of fragments of bark and twigs, something was glowing. Like the embers of a campfire as they fizz away into the summer sky. Ash. Burning. It was here.

The loose swirling metamorphosed into a tight column of air, a vortex which glowed more with every revolution as the ash set the other ingredients aflame. The howling was deafening now, and unlike any storm I have ever heard. It was almost animal. Enes placed a hand on my shoulder and squeezed.

"For Özgur!" he shouted over the din.

I nodded and we strode purposefully toward the burning tornado.

As we got closer to the vortex, the rotation slowed, the outer edges expanding in all directions. Enes reached out an arm to stop me and I paused, watching as the flames dimmed to a grey brown, the particles filling out into a shape familiar from the shadow which had obscured the sun at Tunis airport, what seemed like a lifetime ago.

The hyena.

I'd never seen a hyena in real life before that day, but the proportions of the beast were surely distorted. The shoulders of its front legs stood level with the highest point of the collapsed building behind it. Its head, too, was oversized, its eyes like giant black marbles which seemed to absorb all light. Its mouth was lined with rows of teeth, standing like yellow knives. And in its gullet was the golden glow of the embers from which it had taken form.

It panted, mouth open, tongue lolling to one side and ears twitching as it took us both in.

"You have no idea what you have done." A grotesque, multi-tonal voice, fractured by gravel, spoke the words directly into my head. I turned to Enes and the expression on his face told me the same had happened to him.

"You gave us no choice," I said, the ghost town now silent once again. "I just have one thing I want to ask before we do this. Why Oz? Why?"

The hyena lifted one of its heavy paws and licked the underside nonchalantly. Then: "Why not? Thousands of years in this place. What purpose do you pathetic apes serve if not entertainment?"

"Soysuz!" Enes screamed, the veins pulling taught in his throat and tears streaking his flushed face. His expression hardened and he stepped forward, breaking into a run. I called out for him to wait but either he didn't hear me, or he ignored me. He raised the machete as he had so many times while practising that morning and leaned into the swing with his body, slicing into the hyena's foreleg.

The thing wailed, the sound like a rasping metallic cat cry, then effortlessly smashed a gargantuan paw into Enes' chest, sending him flying backward. He thumped to the ground on his back. My eyes were still on Enes's squirming form when I felt the rumble of the hyena barrelling toward me underfoot. It leapt forward, its uninjured paw held aloft, claws like obsidian daggers slicing through the air toward me.

I darted to one side, lifting my machete above my head in defence. It howled once more as the blade bit into the soft pads underfoot, but the force of the blow slammed me into the wall of a nearby building. I winced as pain juddered through my shoulder, but forced myself onward, out of the path of the thing as it came again.

I ducked and entered one of the more intact houses, leaning against the wall beside the doorway and catching my breath. I peeked around the edge of the doorframe to see Enes scrambling to his feet, blood streaking down in front of his ear from his hair.

Not wanting to expose myself for too long, I made myself small, hugging the corner of the single-roomed building. I heard it breathing and sniffing before I saw anything. Then an oversized foreleg reached around the doorway and began prodding toward me, claws extended, a colossal cat taunting its prey.

I gripped the machete, trying to find space to attack in the poky room. Then the thing shrieked so loudly the walls trembled. The extended limb disappeared from the room in the blink of an eye, and Enes screamed.

I bolted from the house and found Enes on his back, the hyena pinning him with both paws, shaking its head from side to side, spraying vivid red blood in all directions as it chewed down on a chunk of flesh from Enes' arm.

The hyena, too, was wounded. Enes' blade was buried deep in the rump of the thing, between its short, fluffy tail and its right rear leg. A viscous black liquid seeped from around the blade. I was still transfixed by the colourless goo when the beast flicked back its head, swallowing down the meat from Enes' arm. It reared up, ready to strike again. Acting on instinct, I clutched the handle of the stuck blade and heaved back on it with all my strength. The flesh resisted, but the machete slid out of the wound. More black filth evacuated the incision and the thing turned to me, snarling, teeth bared.

Deniz crept out from behind the old church, gesturing for me not to make a sound. She held Enes under his armpits and began to drag him away from the scene.

"Come on, you ancient piece of shit! We've got you! You're finished!" I shouted, thumping the gore-slathered blade onto the stone ground. It cocked its head, snorting through flared nostrils, then paced toward me, straightening up to its full height.

I felt the heat of its breath and knew it was too close. I glanced beyond it and, seeing that Deniz had managed to drag Enes beyond the wall of the church, I stepped back, turning before breaking into a run. I darted between the old school building and a row of houses beside it, hoping the space was too small for the beast to fit.

I glanced over my shoulder and couldn't see it, so allowed myself to slow. My heart hammered in my chest as I looked one way, then the other, along the narrow alleyway between the buildings. A crash sounded above me. A shadow covered the blue sky and those black eyes peered down into the space, watching me.

I froze, paralysed by fear. The space beyond the alley was wide open, no cover for me to stay out of its way. Yet time was running out, the invocation sure to expire, allowing it to dissolve back into the ether.

I took a breath and bolted back the way I'd come.

The sounds of scratching and scrambling followed along the church roof overhead, but I couldn't stop. I had to get out there and face it down. I emerged into the blazing light of the fully risen sun. I spun as I hit the middle of the old village square and looked up as the hyena pounced down from the roof, barrelling into me and sending me flying backward into the doors of the church.

The wooden portal shuddered in its frame as my shoulder smashed into it. I slumped onto to the ancient stone steps, still clutching the knife in one hand. I held it in front of me in an approximation of self-defence, but could feel the fight sapping from my limbs. The beast lumbered forward, dragging its rear leg where Enes had planted his blade. It backed onto its haunches then charged, the muscular bulk of its body pounding against me.

A sharp pain tore through my upper body and I cried out. It stepped backward, snarling through bared teeth. Then it came again. As it slammed into me, something tore in my chest, my muscles tightening, breathing close to impossible. The creature backed up once more, lowered itself onto its haunches, ready to finish me off.

"Hey, fuckface!" Deniz was on top of a collapsed building, next to the church. As the hyena turned its head, she squeezed the trigger and the sound of the rifle shot echoed across the hillside.

In what felt like slow motion, one of its obsidian eyes exploded with the same inky goop that poured from the stab wound at its rear. The beast wailed in a voice that was almost human, its head crashing to the ground, great paws covering the ruined eye. Seeing my chance, I dragged myself up to my knees, searing pain burning through me. I held the machete high above my head, aimed and drove it down through the other, exposed eye. Hot, black blood oozed from the socket, onto my legs and torso. The creature shrieked again.

"Seb, out of the way." Deniz bolted another round into the chamber. I threw myself to one side, as far from the beast's head as I could manage. The thing lifted its head, swinging it blindly, one way, then the other, the shrieking now drawn out into a low groan. A second shot rang out and the bullet drove into the skull of the great thing. It collapsed, silenced.

Not wanting to take any chances, I hauled myself back to one knee, leaned in and placed the cutting edge of the machete along the hyena's neck, and sawed into it. When the blade got stuck, I lifted my foot and brought it down as hard as I could onto the blunt edge, the head detaching and rolling to the ground, heavy, black blood pumping rhythmically from the open neck.

I looked down at my chest, to where the burning pain was worst, and saw blood seeping through my thin shirt. I brought my hand to it, and it came away slick with red.

I passed out.

# Chapter Twenty-One

I came round in the hospital with three ribs broken and another two cracked on the other side. The doctors feared my lung would have been punctured, too, but somehow I'd avoided that. Deniz had been at my bedside throughout the twelve hours I'd been asleep. I was going to be in a lot of pain, but I was also going to be free to leave within a couple days.

Enes wasn't so lucky.

The djinn's monstrous incarnation had taken the flesh almost to the bone on his left arm. He was fortunate it was the outside of his forearm, so no veins or arteries were severed, but he was still facing several rounds of painful and expensive skin grafts. Not to mention not being able to work on the farm for almost a whole season.

Though he protested strongly, I offered to stay on and work in his place. It was the least I could do in the situation. Deniz ended up taking a sabbatical from her position at the university. So, after a few days in Istanbul tying up loose ends, she came back down to Anatolia to help me out.

Marie continued renting the guest apartment for the first few months but closed the café bar. She couldn't face dealing with people every day. And it had always been Oz's baby. When autumn began to turn to winter, she moved up to her and Oz's cabin in the mountains, further north. She went back to photography, putting the apartment up for sale.

With the harvest complete, and Enes having enough strength in his arm to begin the planting for the spring crops, Deniz and I returned to her Istanbul apartment, on the edge of the Galata district.

As I unpacked my things, a flash of blue caught my eye. I tugged at the fabric and the curse script unravelled from the bottom of my case. I quaked as I stared at the brownish stain of Oz's blood, smeared across some of the writing.

"This is the only written copy of this curse, right?"

"As far as I know. No-one else has dared give it physical shape since," Deniz said, cross-legged in her armchair, holding a book in her lap.

"Good." I marched to the kitchen. I clicked on the stove and held the strip of fabric until it caught. I tossed the burning fabric onto the tiled floor and watched it curl and blacken to a pile of charred dust.

"Better?" she said from the doorway.

I shrugged. "Not really. Maybe never."

She clasped her arms around my waist and pressed her body to mine.

"He loved you. And he knew you loved him."

I turned to face her, planted a kiss on her lips. "I hope so."

"I know so. Maybe one day, you'll meet again?"

"Insh'allah?" I said.

"Insh'allah."

# Epilogue

It's been almost two years since those events dragged my friends and I across Turkey and North Africa. Things being what they are in Turkey politically, Deniz and I have settled, for now at least, back at my apartment in north London. This week, though, we're on the road. And, for once, it's not for my work, but for hers. We're in Fez, Morocco.

Five months ago, a team of workmen were digging up the road near the mausoleum of the legendary saint Moulay Idriss to lay new, more efficient water pipes. While they were at it, they happened upon a crypt.

A crypt *beneath* the crypt.

There are somewhere around a dozen burials, but what made them call Deniz in to take a look was the frieze of classical Arabic, carved into the marble along the rear wall. The Moroccan archaeological team initially thought the inscription was lifted from the Quranic account of the day of judgement but, somewhere around halfway, the text deviates.

As soon as I saw her face as she took the call, I could see her interest was piqued. That sparkle in her eyes, and the way the dimple on her right cheek betrays her smile, no matter how hard she fights to keep a straight face.

She's been at the site all morning while I lazed in bed and ate a leisurely breakfast on the roof terrace of our riad. She's covered in pale, sandy dust as she climbs to street level with Mostafa, her local contact.

"So, what do you think?" I ask, offering her a hand up and instantly regretting it as I feel the grime embed itself in every groove of my skin.

"It's …" She looks at Mostafa, then back at me. "*Totally* unique. There are sections of the text which mirror the judgement day account, but others which seem to be about … well … something else entirely. It's beautiful, but heretical at best. Maybe even concerning at worst."

"Concerning how?" I say and offer Mostafa a nod and a wave, which he returns.

"It's hard to say … I just have this idea it's almost like it's not about *us*?"

"Us, as in Muslims?"

"As in *people*."

"Hmmm."

"But there are some interesting fabric pieces down there. Glass and scrolls, too, all with inscriptions." She beams with excitement at this announcement. "Anyway, Seb, Mostafa's invited us to have lunch at a place he knows in the heart of the Medina. I need to go to the bathroom and get washed up first but, what do you say?"

I gaze down the covered street as people mill in all directions, carrying wares to sell or things they've just bought.

"Seb?"

I shake my head. "Sorry. Sounds great. I've not long had breakfast, but I'm on holiday, why not?"

Mostafa offers me a toothy grin.

***

As we mosey from the restaurant, I don't envy Deniz or her supervisor an afternoon of subterranean work. As if reading my mind, Deniz speaks up.

"What are you going to do with yourself this afternoon, mister?"

"Oh, I don't know. Find a tea house. Make inroads into the book I've just started reading. Maybe some baklava if I get peckish."

She leans in to kiss me, then says, "I wish I'd never asked. Have fun."

As I open my eyes, I see two short shadows flit from the work site, thirty yards or so behind Deniz.

"Hey," I say. "What are those kids doing?"

"Kids?" Deniz turns around and, seeing the children sprinting off down an alleyway, fires a volley of quickfire Arabic toward Mostafa, of which I understand only the word 'yalla' – 'hurry.'

I look at the old fellow for a heartbeat before I realise he's got little to no chance of catching the children. "Be right back," I say and sprint after them.

We dart through tunnel-like alleyways and side streets, the scent of the mudbrick impressively vivid considering they're likely a millennium or more old. The kids—a boy and a girl I can see now—use their slight frames and intimate knowledge of the place to stay one step ahead, though I manage to see a wisp of something thin and greenish flowing from the boy's hand.

They scurry left and I follow, narrowly avoiding a pyramid of stacked pottery. The owner castigates first the children, then me. Left again and I realise I have no idea where we are, completely lost in the rabbit warren of narrow streets.

They duck down a crumbling stone staircase, then through a covered jewellery market. I take the steps three at a time, gaining on them, as they scamper up to street level at the other side. I see Deniz and Mostafa, backs turned.

"Deniz, here!"

She spins on her heels and charges at the children, who skid to a halt on the damp cobblestones. A quickfire exchange flies from the girl to the boy and back again in an indecipherable mix of French and Arabic and the boy grasps the ribbon-like object in front of him in both hands. He begins to read.

To begin with, it sounds like a prayer, but then something about the sound, or perhaps the rhythm of the words, strikes me as familiar. The look of sheer horror on Deniz's face tells me she feels it, too.

*The curse.*

"Stop," she cries out. "Halas!" Deniz stalks toward them, reaching for the strip of fabric in the boy's hands. He turns his body, a smile playing across his lips, as though he's playing a game. Finally, she reaches it and tugs it away from him.

But it's too late. He's already finished.

A breeze flows down the winding corridor of streets, carrying with it a whisper.

# Afterword

The first scenes of the book you've just read were real. It all played out just the way I wrote it, up to and including the curious, inexplicable incident with the (very heavy) ice cream trolley.

This was in 2011, when I lived in Turkey for several months for my first overseas teaching job. I knew I had to do something with it, but I carried this story around for about a decade before putting it onto paper.

Part of the reason for that is that the story had to mature from what was, mercifully, a bizarre coincidence which triggered my friend's superstition, into the sprawling, horrifying adventure you find here in this book. The other part was that sense of wanting, needing to get this story right.

I've written from the myths and folklore of others before. The use of the Baba Yaga figure in *The Balance* and the short story, 'Haldjas,' based around a mythological creature from Estonia are just two examples.

With *Shadow*, though, I was stepping into a world where I was the 'other' in a much more dramatic sense. On one hand, I was able to draw on extensive experience of living and travelling in the region—indeed, all the places mentioned in the book are places I've personally visited or lived. But, on the other hand, I was taking an entity from another culture and totally different religious background. So, while this is fiction, and I have at times stretched and contorted the folklore around the djinn to suit my narrative, I wanted to ensure that I had a solid grasp of the lore to work from.

Like with grammar rules in writing: learn the rules well so that you know when and how you're breaking them (if that's what you want to do).

Where, then, to start with developing my understanding of the djinn?

By happy coincidence, just as I was starting to think about this story and how to shape the book, a lawyer and podcaster of Pakistani American origin, Rabia Chaudry released a brilliant podcast series called *The Hidden Djinn*. This was a mixture of personal anecdotes, societal ideas, and notions about the djinn, what they represent, where they supposedly come from and much more. An absolutely vital resource.

What was even better was that the sources she referenced in the show were all collated in the show notes for each episode, so I was able to do further reading. The 2011 book, *The Vengeful Djinn* by Guiley and Imbrogno, in particular, provided a great insight into beliefs around their intentions and the reasons behind their interactions with humans, especially the more negative or hostile ones. There were other highly useful tomes and articles highlighted too.

I also wanted to give Seb, as the protagonist, agency, but not make him the all-knowing white European guy, here to save the day. This is where Deniz, the brilliant Turkish scholar, (and to a lesser extent, Tunisian museum director Ibrahim) comes in. Her experience in the United States means that she straddles the two worlds of East and West and I think (hope) that the book successfully manages that juggling act of ensuring that neither of them would make it without the other.

As you likely noticed, the spirits of fire and air are not yet finished with Seb and Deniz, and I hope you will look forward, as I do, to joining them on the next stage of this adventure.

# ACKNOWLEDGEMENTS

As always with a novel, the author is only one part of a host of people responsible for the final product.

First, I'd like to thank my Turkish friend who lived the beginnings (and, mercifully, not the endings) of Oz's story. His granting permission to use his experience as a jumping-off point is massively appreciated and will not be forgotten. Thanks also to my old student (who also wished to remain nameless) who read the book for sensitivity (and even refused payment!) as well as showing great patience while providing me with modern Turkish words for playful insults and affectionate terms between lovers.

A massive thank you, of course, to Heather and Steve at Brigids Gate Press, for understanding what this story is about and wanting to bring it to readers.

Thanks, too, to my beta readers, Stephanie Ellis, Dan Howarth and Grant Longstaff, all great writers and people without whose insight, *Shadow* would be half the book it is today. On that note, thanks, too, to my better half, Ana: constant first reader, listener to half-baked, often nonsensical ideas at dinners and more.

Thanks, too, to all my fellow writers, readers, bookstagrammers, bloggers, podcasters and others who have lent me their support in my writing career thus far. It is appreciated more than I can ever express.

And finally, thank you to the peoples of the countries explored in this book. For their warm welcome, their food, and their stories. Shukran. I will most definitely be back.

# About the Author

Kev Harrison is a British writer of horror and dark fiction, living in Lisbon, Portugal with his better half, Ana. In addition to *Shadow of the Hidden*, he is the writer novellas, *Below* and *The Balance*, and a short fiction collection, *Paths Best Left Untrodden*. When not plotting his characters' untimely demise, he can be found running, eating, travelling and singing bizarre songs to his cats.

# About the Artist

Mustapha Design DZ is a Graphic Designer & Illustrator, specializing in album covers, movie posters, book covers and merchandise designs...etc; mainly working in the music industry but likes to work on all kinds of artistic projects with a passion for everything that is related to art.

# CONTENT WARNINGS

Animal mutilation
Possession
Suicide

# More From Brigids Gate Press

# BELOW

## BY KEV HARRISON

Decades after his grandfather was buried alive in a Californian gold mine, Dr. Nick Jones teams up with an adventure travel influencer to venture underground and film a documentary, telling the story of what really happened.

What should be a dream come true soon becomes a nightmare as someone or some*thing* stirs ... BELOW.

# THE WOLF AND THE FAVOUR

## BY CATHERINE MCCARTHY

Ten-year-old Hannah has Down syndrome and oodles of courage, but should she trust the alluring tree creature who smells of Mamma's perfume or the blue-eyed wolf who warns her not to enter the woods under any circumstance?

The Wolf and the Favour is a tale of love, trust, and courage. A tale that champions the neurodivergent voice and proves the true power of a person's strength lies within themselves.

# The Five Turns of the Wheel

## by Stephanie Ellis

*Welcome to the Weald. The Five Turns of the Wheel has begun. With each Turn, blood will be spilled, and sacrifices will be made. Pacts will be made … and broken. Will you join the Dance?*

In the Weald, the time has come for the Five Turns of the Wheel. Tommy, Betty and Fiddler, the sons of Hweol, Lord of Umbra, have arrived to oversee the sacred rituals … rituals brimming with sacrifice and dripping with blood.

Megan Wheelborn, daughter of Tommy, hatches a desperate plan to free the people of the Weald from the bloody and cruel grip of Umbra, and put an end to its murderous rituals. But success will require sacrifice and blood as well. Will Megan be able to pay the price?

# A Man in Winter

## by Katie Marie

'A mesmerizing psychological mystery from an author who brings a refreshing new voice to horror. This is a quick read, but one that keeps the reader thoroughly intrigued and entertained from beginning to end.'

—Catherine Cavendish, author of *In Darkness, Shadows Breathe* and *Dark Observation* (coming in September 2022)

Arthur, whose life was devastated by the brutal murder of his wife, must come to terms with his diagnosis of dementia. He moves into a new home at a retirement community, and shortly after, has his life turned upside down again when his wife's ghost visits him and sends him on a quest to find her killer so her spirit can move on. With his family and his doctor concerned that his dementia is advancing, will he be able to solve the murder before his independence is permanently restricted?

*A Man in Winter* examines the horrors of isolation, dementia, loss, and the ghosts that come back to haunt us.

Visit our website at: www.brigidsgatepress.com